HER STRANDED BILLIONAIRE MIX-UP

A CLEAN BILLIONAIRE ROMANCE BOOK FIVE

BREE LIVINGSTON

Edited by
CHRISTINA SCHRUNK

Her Stranded Billionaire Mix-Up

Copyright © 2018 by **Bree Livingston**

Edited by Christina Schrunk

https://www.facebook.com/christinaschrunk.editor

Proofread by Krista R. Burdine

https://www.facebook.com/iamgrammaresque

Cover design by Victorine Lieske

http://victorinelieske.com/

All rights reserved. No part of this publication may be reproduced, distributed or transmitted in any form or by any means, without prior written permission.

Bree Livingston

https://breelivingstonwrit.wixsite.com/breelivingston

Publisher's Note: This is a work of fiction. Names, characters, places, and incidents are a product of the author's imagination. Locales and public names are sometimes used for atmospheric purposes. Any resemblance to actual people, living or dead, or to businesses, companies, events, institutions, or locales is completely coincidental.

Her Stranded Billionaire Mix-Up / Bree Livingston. -- 1st ed.

ISBN: 9781983284496

Thanks for sticking with me! I appreciate all your encouragement and kind words.

Thanks to my family for giving me the time to write, even though it's summer.

And heartfelt thanks to my editor and proofreader who helped make this book better than it started out.

CHAPTER 1

With a clipboard in hand, Zachary Wolf inspected the aircraft he'd be flying. Well, he was trying to inspect it, but his mind kept wandering. He had so many things to do. This trip to Jamaica to drop off equipment to his friend Matt needed to go off without a hitch.

With a new company looking for a computer parts distributor, it was Zach's job to convince them to use the Wolf company. He didn't trust anyone else to do it. The last time he'd trusted someone, they'd nearly cost the company a client and millions of dollars.

His phone buzzed in his pocket, and he pulled it out, sandwiching it between his shoulder and his ear.

"Hey, Zach!"

Hearing his sister's voice was a relief. "Hey, Britney." Hopefully, she was calling with news about the fill-in assistant he needed. His current assistant, Nathan, had picked the worst time to call in sick. But Zach really couldn't complain. Nathan was great and hardly ever missed a day, so he must not be feeling great.

"Getting things ready?" she asked.

"Trying. I keep getting distracted." He made sure his tone was playful.

"Har har. I guess if you don't want to know about the assistant, I'll just talk to you later."

"You got someone?"

"Yeah, someone's coming." He could see the grin on her face. She'd set him up again.

"What did you do?"

"Nothing."

"Brit," he said, his tone holding an edge.

"I promise I didn't do anything. The agency is sending someone with tons of experience, just like you asked."

"Male, right?"

She was quiet for too long. "No, but she's older. Like, way older. In her fifties."

"Why don't I believe you?"

"Because you have trust issues stemming from

childhood trauma due to your parents going through a divorce?"

He took a deep breath and rolled his eyes. "You better not be setting me up. I'm not interested in a relationship."

"But you need someone, Zach. You're lonely. I know you are."

Zach let the clipboard in his hand fall to his side as he took his phone in his hand. "I'm fine. I have friends, and they keep me plenty happy."

"I know what happened with Mom and Dad was hard, but you're not Dad. And if you'd give Mom just a second to talk to you—"

He set the clipboard down as his anger bubbled. "No. There is no excuse for the way he treated Mom. And he deserved what he got."

"He was—"

"No," he said, his tone so firm it was nearly biting.

Britney stayed quiet a minute. "Message received."

"Thank you. I *don't* want to be in a relationship. Not now, not ever. If I did, I have plenty of options. I don't need you interfering."

His phone beeped, and he pulled it from his ear. "Oh, hey, that's Matt. I need to go."

"But I need—"

"Sorry, Brit, gotta go." He touched the screen and answered his friend. "Hey."

Matt yelled something that Zach couldn't make out and then said, "Hey, I was calling so I know what time you'll be here."

"Before dinner, I hope. I'm waiting on a temp assistant to get here."

"Another working vacation?"

Zach shrugged. "I can't help it."

"You own the company, so that excuse doesn't fly," Matt said. He was a good man and an even better friend, but Zach never had a conversation with him that didn't involve a lecture about Zach's work habits.

"You know how it is."

"What I know is that you need a change. I know the way you're living is stressful, and if you don't take a break soon, you're going to run yourself down."

Zach took a deep breath. No one seemed to understand him. If he could trust people, sure, it'd be great to take a break. Why couldn't people understand that? His mom, brothers, sisters…none of them got it. "Are you calling to lecture me or to find out about the equipment?"

"Fine. Tell me."

"It's a state-of-the-art anesthesia machine."

Matt gasped. "You managed to talk the guy into it?"

It'd taken so much schmoozing, Zach had nearly thrown up, but he'd managed to convince the CEO of Regent Medical Technology to let him buy their newest not-on-the-market-yet machine. "No."

"What? No?"

"No, I got two."

"Two? Oh man, I can get another doctor over here."

Matt never intended to stay in Jamaica when he first volunteered as a cleft palate surgeon, but the need in the area for a surgeon had been so great that he'd moved there. He'd quickly come back to the States, closed his practice, and returned. Zach respected him for that. There weren't many people who would give up their life of luxury to do what he did.

"I've never kissed up so much in my life, but yeah, I got two of them. I even have more surgical supplies."

"I don't know how I'll ever repay you."

"You don't have to. I want to do this. How's the school going?"

Matt exhaled sharply. "It's good. It's been finished since you were here last. Kids are starting to come, and they're doing so well."

"Is Heather loving it?" Matt's wife was a teacher. If anyone could ever convince him that a relationship had the ability to go the distance, it was Matt and

Heather. Their relationship was so strong that it sometimes made him wish he hadn't sworn them off.

Matt chuckled. "Yeah, she's in heaven. Those kids are so bright. You have no idea the impact you're having."

"You should find someone to love," Heather called out. Matt had him on speaker phone. Great. Now both of them were going to be chewing on him. "There's a woman out there who needs what you have to offer, Zachary Wolf."

Zach didn't respond.

"You know I'm right. Tell him I'm right, Matt."

Matt laughed. "Okay, she's right, but that's not how I would have said it."

"Yeah, yeah," Zack said. "Hey, let me get this inspection done or I'll never get there."

"You're a chicken!" Heather called.

"Bye, you two."

"Bye!"

He ended the call and picked up his clipboard again. The next week would be filled with Matt gushing about the new equipment and Heather arguing with him about his relationship status. Neither of which made him comfortable.

He donated the equipment because of how good it made him feel. That was enough. He didn't want a relationship, no matter how many people thought he did. Going to Jamaica was great, but Zach was getting tired of the "love" talks.

Love didn't work. His parents had proven that. Well, no, his dad had proven that with how awful he treated his mom. One day his dad was a loving man who treated all of them like they were valued, and the next, he was someone Zach didn't recognize.

That's not what he wanted, and if that's how thirty years of loving someone ended, Zach wanted no part of it.

WITH A LONG SIGH, Harley parked her car and cut the engine in front of the private hangar near the George Bush Intercontinental Airport. The tension between her shoulders was building to the point where she thought they'd snap. It was just another interview—emphasis on *another*. Three months without a bite was wearing her thin.

Great. When she'd applied for an office cleaning position, she hadn't expected it to be here. If she had known, there was no way she'd have agreed to the interview. She rolled her eyes as her top lip curled.

People with money. She'd learned the hard way that they were people to avoid.

As an assistant party planner to Trixie Tanner, *the* party planner in Houston, she'd been around her fair share of entitled rich people. The kind who wanted the crusts cut off their sandwiches with gold knives.

It was at one of the first parties she helped plan that she met Samuel Baldwin. He wasn't just from money; he was from old Houston money. They'd only met because one of the waitresses had an issue with her uniform and Harley had filled in for a brief moment. She'd been carrying a tray of champagne, and Samuel thought she was a server. At the time, she was new to Houston and knew him by name only, not face.

He'd been charming and charismatic as he followed her around all night long. After the event was over, he'd asked for her number. Thinking he'd never call, she'd given it to him. Two days later, he surprised her by calling to ask her out. From that moment on, she'd been smitten. He'd taken her to a fantastically hard-to-get-into restaurant, on a carriage ride, and then took her home. He didn't even try to kiss her goodnight.

A tear rolled down her cheek, and she quickly swiped it away. Now wasn't the time to be hobbling down memory lane. She had rent to pay, and she needed a job. If she didn't need it so badly, she'd be putting her car in gear and testing its speed limit in an effort to get away from another situation involving money-hungry people.

She eyed the hangar again, wishing she wasn't so desperate. Hopefully, the man who owned it wasn't a rich snob, but she wasn't holding her breath.

Why had Trixie fired her? Even with a broken heart and being jilted at the altar, Harley had given Trixie her best, and that last party had been a success, just like all of the parties she worked on.

The day Harley was called into Trixie's office, just a month after the called-off wedding, she'd expected a raise or a bonus, only to be given her pink slip. It was like the rotten cherry on a melted sundae. It was the second worst week she'd had since moving to Houston.

Man, she wished her grandma was still alive. She'd know what to do. Of course, her grandma would say to ditch the lease, but with it being in Harley's name, that wasn't an option. She'd need a good credit score when she got back to Lubbock.

Her plan was to move home and start her own party-planning business, which would take loans to get started. If nothing else, working for Trixie had given her the confidence to know she could be successful doing it.

It didn't take the sting out of being left at the altar, but Harley was a Wilson, and Wilson women took what was in front of them and made it work. Which is why she wasn't going to let rich people run her off from this job. Rich people or no, Harley was going to rock this job interview.

CHAPTER 2

Why had she arrived so early? Oh yeah, nerves, according to her sweaty palms. Harley checked the time on her phone. She still had ten minutes before she was expected. The thought hit her that maybe she could check out the inside. Would it hurt to scout it out, just in case? If the person was rich, there'd probably be expensive cars and the like. If so, that'd be her sign to leave. If not, maybe there was a chance the owner was a regular Joe, and she'd at least stay for the interview.

She got out of the car and smoothed her black knee-length pencil skirt down. More than likely, she was overdressed, but that's what her mom taught her. Always do everything with your best foot forward.

Just because it was a menial position didn't mean she couldn't dress nice.

The butterflies in her stomach swirled. She couldn't understand why she was so nervous. It was just a cleaning position. *For someone wealthy.* The year with Samuel had taken its toll. His family, the way they looked at her, how they treated her...and how he ended the relationship made her feel worthless. And now, here she was, about to subject herself to the same potentially snobby attitude, all because she'd lost her job with Trixie. And for some reason, no one else would hire her.

Harley pulled her shoulders back and held her head high. No, this time would be different. She wouldn't let anyone make her feel that way again. Job or no job, she'd tell them where they could stuff it if they were rude. As she reached the hangar, the doors slid open, revealing a small jet. It didn't look much different from Samuel's.

From where she stood, she could see a man with broad shoulders in low-hung jeans and a t-shirt with his back to her. When he turned around, he looked startled for a second before his eyebrows knitted together. Oddly enough, the guy looked familiar, but she couldn't place how. It surprised her because as good-looking as he was, he'd be hard to forget. Being rich, it was possible she'd seen him at an art show.

She smiled as she approached him, thinking he was even better-looking up close. Wow, those eyes—a light blue that almost felt like a flashlight for the soul. And what kind of cologne was that? Ode de lady killer?

"Hi. I'm—"

"I told her I wanted a male assistant." He exhaled sharply and pulled out his phone. "I guess it is what it is. I don't have time to wait while they send another replacement."

Well, wasn't that a needle scratching the record. Harley felt like she'd been smacked. A male assistant? Like a woman couldn't do the job? And assistant? Hadn't she applied for a cleaning job? Maybe she got them mixed up. She'd applied for so many that it was hard to keep them straight. "I thought—"

A puzzled look crossed his face. "Where's your luggage? This is a week-long trip."

"I—"

"Do you have luggage or not?"

"I thought I had to interview for the job."

The man pinched the bridge of his nose. "Great. That's the last time I trust Britney with getting a replacement anything."

Harley raised an eyebrow. First, he wanted a male

assistant, and now he was complaining about a woman. His good looks had taken a serious nose dive. Chauvinist pig. She leaned back, ready to lower the verbal boom on the guy, when he softened.

"I'm sorry. It's just been a long week. I don't mean to take it out on you. I asked my sister to find a temporary assistant. I love her, but she likes to meddle."

Harley took a deep breath. Okay, so not just because she was a woman, but because she was his sister. She started to ask what he meant by *meddle* when he held up his hand.

"Don't ask," he said.

"Okay."

"Is there any chance you can travel for a week?" He swore under his breath. "I have to get to Jamaica, and I can't wait for someone else to show up."

She thought about the next rent due date, and it took a second to decide. It was just a week. "Will it pay the same?"

"I'll throw in a bonus if you'll go." He raked his hand through his hair. "Do you have clothes?"

He had her at bonus. "Actually, yeah, I do. I just got back from my mom's late last night. I'll need the use of a washer and dryer when I get there."

He stuck his hand out to her. "Deal."

"And the bonus?"

"Will ten grand get you on that plane?"

Harley resisted the urge to pass out. Ten thousand? Holy smokes. She'd have been happy with a couple. With that much, it'd give her the ability to pay out the rest of her lease *and* move back home. Was it worth it to put up with a rich guy? Totally.

She grinned and shook his hand. "Deal."

"Fantastic. Get your luggage, and let's go."

ZACHARY SHUT the door to the plane and wheeled around. He should have known what Britney was up to when she told him the agency was sending a woman. That was the last time he trusted Brit. When he got back from Jamaica, they'd be having a talk about her interference in his love life.

He took a deep breath to calm himself. It wasn't this woman's fault his sister was a busybody, and he shouldn't take it out on her. And he'd been in such a hurry he'd completely forgotten to introduce himself. "I'm Zachary Wolf."

"Harley Wilson," she said as she took her seat, crossing her incredibly long legs at the ankles.

He shook his head. Nope. Her legs could circle the globe, and he still wouldn't be interested. Relationships only brought pain and heartache. The divorce his parents' were going through before his father's death was enough to swear him off relationships and women for life.

"Harley? Should I sleep with one eye open?" He grinned, thinking about the comic book character.

She shook her head and chuckled. "No." Her laugh was bubbly with a genuine feel to it. And despite his arm's-length approach to the opposite sex, his heart raced. Man, she was beautiful, with a pair of the most kissable pouty lips he'd ever seen. Her hair was pulled back in a bun, but he pictured it long and soft. He shook his head. Nope, no kissable lips or silky hair or anything else.

"Good to know." For some unknown reason, he sat across from her. He wasn't necessarily in a hurry, but he didn't have time to just sit, either. "Although, I don't think it'd be a chore to keep an eye on you." Where had that come from? Flirting was not part of the plan. He never flirted with women.

A blanket of the most perfect pink blush settled over her cheeks. He couldn't tell if she was embarrassed or offended. What was he doing? Looking for a sexual harassment suit? "I'm sorry. That was my inexperienced way of a…well…" How on earth did he get himself out of this mess? "I'm just sorry."

She pointed her gaze at the floor, as if she was looking at his shoes, and tilted her head.

He lifted his feet, wondering what she couldn't possibly be looking at. "What?"

"Just thinking those are nice shoes. I mean, if you're going to put your foot in your mouth, might as well do it while wearing good shoes."

Zach laughed. "You think you're funny, but that's precisely why I chose them. I've come to know which brand tastes the best, unfortunately."

Her shoulders bounced as she covered her mouth with her hand, her cheeks lifting enough to show a crease in the corners of her eyes.

Clearing his throat and deciding he needed a change of topic, he said, "You don't look like you're in your fifties." Maybe he'd remembered wrong.

She chuckled again. "Uh, no. I'm twenty-seven."

Yeah, that's what he thought. It *was* a setup. Harley was three years younger than him. *Britney!*

"It seemed like you were in a rush to get out of Houston," she said.

He shook his head. "No, not really. I just don't have time to wait for someone else."

"The other person would just need to drive here."

Zach looked at his phone. "It's morning rush hour. There's no way they could make it in time for takeoff."

"Oh." She tilted her head. "Where's the pilot?"

"That'd be me."

"Do you own this plane?"

Zach laughed. What a joke. The only reason he still had it was because of his trips to take supplies and equipment to Matt. If it weren't for the humanitarian aspect, he'd sell the jet in a heartbeat. It had been his father's, and Zach hated the thing. "My family does. It was purchased before I took over the company."

"You said your last name was Wolf? That name sounds familiar."

He was sure it did, and since he'd taken over, he'd made it even more successful than his father. "I own the largest computer component and parts distribution company in the country, Wolf Computer C & D Distribution."

Her eyes widened. "I think I saw an interview…the billionaire."

Billionaire. He hated it. No, that was a lie. He liked having the money because of what he could do with it. It was the other side of having money that he hated. Always being on guard because he never knew if someone liked him or his money.

"My father, before he died," he said, biting back the bitterness he felt. As his father aged, they'd fought over and over, not just about the money but how he treated people.

As a kid, his dad had been a friend to everyone, but by the end, anyone associated with the Wolf's needed to have money. If they didn't, they weren't people the Wolf's needed to associate with.

Zach's mom was the polar opposite of his dad. He never understood why his father changed so much the last few years of his life. Then again, Zach didn't care because there was no excuse.

Her gaze held his, and her eyes grew stormy for a heartbeat before she said, "Oh, I'm sorry."

Zach nearly sighed in relief. And he wasn't sorry about his dad. Their relationship was non-existent by the time he died. "Don't be." He cleared his throat. "So, you want to sit back here or in the co-pilot's seat?"

"You'd let me sit up there?"

He laughed. "Promise not to hijack the plane?"

She chuckled. "I would really like to not crash, and if I hijack this plane, that's exactly what will happen."

Beautiful with a side of humor. He liked that. With a smile, he tipped his chin toward the front of the plane. "I've got a pre-flight check, and then we can put Houston in the rearview mirror." He paused a second. "You'll need to put your phone on airplane mode until we're in the air, okay?"

"Okay." Harley pulled her phone out, tapped a couple of buttons, and put it back.

Zach stood and waited for Harley. "We should be there before dinner."

"And we're there for a week?"

"Right," he said and sat in the pilot's seat.

"I assume you're doing business in Jamaica." Harley glanced around the cockpit and sat.

Zachary studied her a moment. It almost felt like she'd been in a cockpit before, but she'd seemed surprised by his offer. He waved it off as ridiculous. Most likely, she was just trying to look confident. If that was the case, she was pulling it off well. "Uh, no. Actually, I have a friend who runs a small clinic down there. I've got some equipment I'm donating so it's easier for him."

Her lips twitched at the corners. "That's...really kind of you."

He'd seen that type of smile before. It was the kind that gave him attention he didn't want. Did he set her straight now or later? Later, definitely. They weren't off the ground yet, and if he made her mad, there was a good chance she'd leave him high and dry. Besides, he didn't know her. *Maybe* she was being genuine. He'd just watch the flirting to make sure it didn't happen again.

"Why do you need an assistant if you're not going there for business?" she asked.

He exhaled softly. "It's a working vacation. I'm taking him the equipment then working most of the time."

"Oh. Do you always work on vacation?"

"No, but I have responsibilities now that I've taken over the company, and I'm more comfortable taking care of it myself." He really had tried to trust people, but without fail, they'd disappoint him every time. He'd yet to meet anyone who didn't lie to get what they wanted from him.

She nodded. "Oh, okay."

Silence settled between them as Zach finished with his pre-flight checks and started the engines of the plane. He taxied out of the hangar and onto the runway, and in minutes, he had them in the air.

His father was the main factor in learning to fly. The sky was the only way to escape the man when he was alive. Zach was supposed to carry on the Wolf name in the same manner his father had, but Zach didn't like how the Wolf name was now associated with elitism and selfishness. Once his father died, he'd made it his life's goal to give back. Wealth didn't have to mean heartless behavior.

When he reached cruising altitude, Zach leaned his

head back against the seat. "This is my favorite place to be."

"It is peaceful."

Zach waited a few beats and figured it'd be a good idea to get to know her at least a little since they had to work together for the coming week. "So, are you from Houston?"

"No, I grew up in Lubbock."

He gave her a quick glance. "Wow, you're far from home."

"Yeah."

"What brought you here in the first place?"

"I wanted a change."

She folded her hands in her lap and stared out the windshield. "Are you from Houston?"

"Yep, born and bred."

He'd lived in Houston his entire life. It was more than his home. He loved the city. The nightlife, the people, the history. There was no other place he'd rather be. Other than maybe San Antonio. He'd fallen in love with that city too. Enough that he'd even purchased a second home there.

"Oh. That's nice." Her clipped tone said it was anything but. He'd be carefully stepping around that topic. "I guess you'd know the Baldwins, then?"

"Yeah, Sam and I are friends. Did you work for

them?" The Baldwins were friends of the family. Zach's family wasn't old money like the Baldwins, but he'd grown up with Samuel, James, and Xavier. Calling them friends was polite. As they'd grown older, Zach had less and less in common with them. They were too much like the senior Wolf—greedy and self-serving.

"You could say that." Her tone was icy.

He glanced at her. Maybe the employment hadn't ended on good terms. "Did you have a problem with them?"

"No. We had a disagreement over my value."

Ah, so it was employment related. Maybe he'd give Sam a call and find out what happened. He hated to do it, but Zach had been burned enough that he never turned down the chance to double check someone.

An uncomfortable silence settled over the cockpit. He was getting a strange vibe from her, like he'd said something wrong. "Um, did I say something that upset you?"

"No, but I do want to make one thing clear. I don't get involved with bosses or billionaires. I'm here to work, and that's it." Her tone held an edge to it.

Well, it seemed he *wouldn't* have to set her straight. She was already there. "I'm fantastic with that. I don't date employees." Or anyone else for that matter.

Harley shot him a side-glance. He nearly shivered; it was so cold. "Then we should get along fabulously."

Zach smiled. "Thanks for helping me out."

"It's a job. Nothing more, nothing less." She stood. "I think I'll sit in the back, if you don't mind."

"Uh, sure. I'll let you know when we're close to landing."

"Thanks." She walked out of the cockpit and took a seat in the chair she'd previously occupied.

He glanced over his shoulder as she walked to her seat. What had happened? They were talking one second, and she was shut down the next. He should have been thrilled, especially when he was having a hard time keeping his eyes off her. But with expectations laid on the table, it'd make things easy. And she'd been the one to lay them out. He may not want anything romantic, but a friendly business relationship would have been nice. Oh well, nothing he could change now.

At least he could concentrate on other things instead of worrying about mixed messages. As long as she did her job, they'd get along great. And there'd be nothing beyond business. This trip would be easy.

CHAPTER 3

If Harley had known Zach was friends with Samuel before the plane got in the air, she'd have demanded to get off. She wanted nothing to do with anyone associated with him. Not for a minute. Bonus or no bonus. If Zach was friends with the Baldwins, more than likely he was just like them. Snobby and cruel. Even the donated medical equipment, which had initially impressed her, was most likely a tax write-off.

Once Zach said he knew the Baldwins, she immediately knew where she'd seen him before. At a Baldwin party. It had been a huge, formal party with fancy dresses and so many people it was stifling. She'd felt so out of place.

Crossing her arms over her chest, she let her gaze

settle on the window and the puffy white clouds that floated past. She leaned her head back on the chair as memories played.

It was her first big party and the first time Samuel had introduced her to his parents. That night she overheard Mr. and Mrs. Baldwin talking to Samuel in hushed tones about his choice in acceptable dates. They made it crystal clear she wasn't. *Where did you pick this one up, Samuel?* It was like she had his mother's voice on recording. *You'll end this now.* Harley Wilson was not only poor, but she wasn't good enough for Samuel or their family. Party planner wasn't a respectable profession, and Harley wasn't suitable for a Baldwin. Samuel just stood there, saying nothing. That should have been enough right there to leave him, but by then, she'd been so smitten.

It baffled Harley at the time. Samuel seemed to be down to earth and kind. He was a grown man, and his parents were telling him who he could date? She'd expected him to take her home and that she'd never hear from him again after that. Why would he risk making his family angry for her?

To her surprise, he called the next day. Samuel didn't care what they thought. It was a whirlwind after that. Dinner, parties, and long romantic weekends to Italy and Paris. Places she'd only dreamed of going.

The whole experience was like a fairytale. He treated her like a princess, with flowers, dancing, and nice restaurants, and she loved every minute of it. At twenty-six, it was the first time she'd been in a relationship she felt had the potential to last. She'd tried so hard to get his parents' approval, but nothing she did ever kept them from looking down their noses at her.

She'd fallen head over heels for him. When he asked her to marry him after six months of dating, she'd nearly tripped over herself to say yes. His parents had nearly passed out. In front of all their snobby friends, Samuel had declared his undying love for her. It'd been amazing.

Samuel didn't want a long engagement, either. Of course, in true male fashion, he left the details to her. Over the next six months, she planned a small, beautiful wedding. To her, it couldn't have been more perfect.

None of it had stopped his parents' objections. No, they'd only become more vocal about his marrying some poor, unknown party planner. But all through their objections, he'd promised he didn't care. That is, until his father told him if he married her, he'd be cut out of the family business.

That's what the note had said. Harley was crushed. The embarrassment she felt was still as strong as it was that day. Samuel didn't even have the guts to tell her to her face.

The wedding march was playing as she was handed the letter.

It'd taken her two months to crawl out of bed. She'd loved him with everything in her, and that should've been enough. But rich people rubbed elbows with rich people. If she'd been smart, she would've walked away the moment she found out who he was, because, in the end, money was all that mattered.

Now that she thought about it, Samuel hadn't introduced her to any of the other guests that night at the party where she saw Zach. Just his parents. At the time, she thought it was Samuel trying to keep her from feeling overwhelmed, but now it made her wonder.

She lifted her gaze, and it landed on Zach. Her stomach churned. He was friends with Samuel. The moment the words left his mouth, it was like toxic waste had been poured over his handsome head.

At first, she'd thought he was attractive. Dark, purposefully tousled hair, light blue eyes—the kind you find on Pinterest and saved to a board called *Smoldering*—and tall. Taller than her, which was saying something because she was five foot eight.

Why did he have to be friends with Samuel? Things

would have been okay if she didn't know that. Now, she was going to be stuck working with the jerk. Although, she didn't know him, and he had seemed nice, at least after he apologized. But Samuel had been nice too, and he'd left her heartbroken.

She'd almost told him she'd dated Samuel when Zach asked if she had a problem with the Baldwins, but it wasn't something she wanted to share with someone she just met, especially given the way her relationship ended. Add to that the fact that Zach was friends with Sam?

Or, maybe he'd have given her the sad look like so many others did when she told them. That response was the worse. Harley Wilson was a lot of things, but she wasn't a charity case. Samuel had crushed her heart. It happened to people all the time and they lived through it. And she survived just fine. Still, she was ashamed, and she wanted to avoid the inevitable question of: why did he leave you?

Because you weren't good enough, flitted through her mind. Harley blinked back tears. Samuel never even called her after he'd left her. When she'd tried to call him, he wouldn't take her calls. Now, she wondered if it wasn't because he was ashamed of her or something. Maybe his parents had finally gotten to him and that was the real reason why he'd dumped her. Being abandoned because of the love of money—or the fear of losing it—was one thing, but to be left because he believed what his parents thought about her was worse.

She pulled her phone out of her purse and took it off airplane mode. A moment later, it vibrated as several texts buzzed through. She'd missed four calls too.

Ms. Wilson, I'm at the hangar waiting for you.

Harley tilted her head, and her eyebrows drew together. Waiting on her? What? When she'd scheduled the interview, she was told that the man who owned the hangar would be interviewing her. She'd been so excited to get a call, she'd hung up before asking who would be interviewing her.

Another text. *Ms. Wilson, am I to assume you've decided not to show for the interview?*

She stood and walked to the cockpit. "Are you the owner of that hangar?"

Zach glanced over his shoulder at her. "No, why?"

Her shoulders sagged. Great. "I think there's been a huge mix-up."

"What?"

"I was at the hangar to interview for an office cleaning job."

He touched a few buttons and turned in the seat. "Office cleaning job?"

"Yeah, I thought you were the owner."

Zach pinched the bridge of his nose. "So, Britney didn't hire you for the assistant position."

"Apparently not, but in my defense, I'd applied for several jobs. When you said assistant, I assumed I'd gotten the interviews confused."

"Great." He huffed.

"I can still do the job." There was no way to make him understand that when she was determined to do something, she did it. Whatever she had to do to get the job done, she'd get it done.

He lifted his gaze to hers. "Can you? How much experience do you have as an assistant?"

Did she tell him the truth? That she'd thrown darts at the job opportunities and applied for what paid well, hoping that her sheer determination helped? She'd been desperate when none of the party planning agencies would hire her. "I have enough." She'd been an assistant party planner. Didn't that count a little?

"That means zero, right?"

"I've never taken a job I can't handle. It can't be that hard."

Zach let out a frustrated sigh. "Fantastic."

She lifted an eyebrow. "I'm not exactly thrilled to

be here either. Had I known…" She stopped short of saying, "Had I known you were friends with Samuel, I wouldn't be here."

"Known what?"

"Nothing."

"When we get to Jamaica, I'll book you a flight home. No offense, but I wanted someone with experience for a reason." His tone was clipped.

Harley crossed her arms over her chest. "Fine. I will happily go back home. I don't want to be stuck with you any more than you want to be stuck with me."

"I'm not the one who accepted a job without having any experience whatsoever."

"No, you aren't, because you don't have to. You don't have to worry about paying your bills like the rest of us commoners. So sorry to *bother* you, your majesty." She spun on her heels and walked back to her seat.

So much for him being different from Baldwins, and her theory had been proven. *All* rich people were jerks who sat in ivory towers, looking down their noses at the rest of the world. The moment they landed in Jamaica, she would gladly get on a plane to get away from the likes of Zachary Wolf.

Harley had learned her lesson. From now on, she'd

find out who was interviewing her and do a google search before showing up to the interview. This was never happening again. Rich people were officially off her "second-chances" list.

Lightning crackled and lit up the swirling dark clouds that stretched endlessly ahead. Zach cursed under his breath. The storm had come out of nowhere. One minute it was baby-blue skies and little puffy clouds, and the next, they were surrounded.

He'd radioed for information, but the storm had caused so much interference that he couldn't understand what he was being told. If he'd turned the plane around, maybe he could've flown ahead of it back to Houston, but he'd chosen to continue to Jamaica. He didn't have enough fuel left to turn around now.

At least when he landed in Jamaica, he'd be rid of Harley Wilson. It wasn't his fault he assumed she was the assistant Britney had hired. Wanting someone experienced wasn't being a jerk. Granted, it wasn't like he asked a lot of questions either. The week had been stressful, and he'd just wanted to get out of Houston.

And commoner? What was that about? When had he treated her like that? As an employee, sure, but not someone beneath him. Zach had never bought into that line of thought. He was a regular guy who happened to have money. Money he wanted to spread around instead of guarding it like it would suddenly disappear. His family had more than enough to live comfortably and still make a difference in people's lives.

The plane bounced and jerked to the right, bringing him back to the current problem. His eyes widened as smoke billowed from one of the engines. Had he been so preoccupied during the inspection that he'd missed something?

"What's happening?" Harley asked as she took the co-pilot's seat.

"We hit some turbulence."

"No, really? I thought I was in a washing machine's spin cycle. I mean, what's with the smoke coming from the engine?"

He shook his head. "I don't know."

"And you were giving me a hard time about applying for a job when I didn't have experience?"

"The only way to know what happened to the engine is to go out there and look at it. I can't exactly do that, now, can I?"

Thunder clapped as lightning flashed through the clouds. Why hadn't he turned around the moment he saw the cloud? The equipment. Matt needed it, and Zach thought he could handle a storm. It didn't seem that bad flying into it, but once inside, it was worse than he could've imagined.

"I've never seen lightning like this before. It's kinda pretty in a we're-gonna-die sort of way." Harley gripped the arms of the seat.

Zach shot her a glance. If he'd just asked a few questions, she wouldn't be in this mess. "Look, I'm really sorry about the way I acted before. I should have asked more questions and not assumed you were from the agency."

"It's okay." She loosened her grip on the chair arm and laid a hand on his forearm. The warmth of her hand sent zings of nerve-wracking electricity across his skin. "I shouldn't let my biases cloud my judgment and then act like I know you. I'm sorry."

They locked eyes, and his mouth went dry. He cleared his throat, trying to loosen his jaw. "I think we're all a little guilty of that at times." His gaze settled on her lips—those perfect lips—and he wondered if they'd be as perfect at kissing as they were to look at.

He pulled his gaze away as he realized she'd caught him staring, and she looked away as a smile crept across her lips.

Geez. Talk about needing to get his priorities straight.

They were literally in a plane going down in flames, and all he could think about was kissing her. I mean, if he was going to die, wouldn't it be better than screaming?

The plane bounced hard and jolted. More smoke poured from the engine.

"Uh, there's smoke coming from this engine too," Harley said as she stared out her window, her grip on his arm tightening.

"I might have to make an emergency landing."

She scoffed. "You don't say."

Zach shot her a quick glance. "Why aren't you freaking out?"

"And that'll accomplish what?"

Wow, he was impressed. Most women would have been screaming their heads off, especially since he wasn't far off from that himself. Maybe he'd been too quick to send her back to Houston. "You have a point."

The plane rocked sideways, and Zach fought to get it level. His heart pounded, and he white-knuckled the controls. The choice was gone. He had to land the plane.

"Did we get hit with lightning?"

"No, I don't think so. I have to land before we fall from the sky with zero control."

Harley let go of his arm to grip the armrests again.

"Okay, but I think you forgot the 'crash' part in front of landing."

Zach shot her a glance and took the plane down low enough that he could make out a few islands in the distance. Which one? If they were stuck for a while, they'd need fresh water and food. His heart sank. What if he picked the wrong one? It wasn't just his life at stake. It was Harley's too. "I—"

Before he could finish, Harley quickly stood, took his face in her hands, and kissed him. Did she read his mind? Or had she been thinking the same thing? Were his lips tingling because of the kiss or from the sudden lack of altitude?

Leaving one hand on the controls, he buried his other in her hair and deepened the kiss. If this was his last kiss, he was going to make it count. Oh man, were her lips soft and sweet. Was that green apple he tasted? It'd been a long time since he'd kissed anyone, and this one was incredible.

Waves of electricity rolled across his skin, sending his pulse racing. He nearly let go of the controls just so he could pull her even closer. He didn't know how well she fit against him, but if her lips were any indication, she'd fit perfectly.

And just as quickly as it started, she pulled back,

wide-eyed and holding his gaze. "If I'm gonna die, may as well go happy, right?"

Heartbeat after heartbeat he just stared at her, dazed and wishing it hadn't ended. If they weren't about to crash, he'd be kissing her again.

The plane shuddered and dipped, bringing him back to reality and making his stomach feel like he was on a rollercoaster. At this point, he'd have to take his chances. Suddenly, he had extra motivation to safely land the plane. Even if it didn't lead to more kissing, he'd quickly realized that maybe relationships weren't as off the table as he thought. Wouldn't it just be his luck, though, to have that epiphany and then crash and burn? Man, the irony.

He pointed the plane toward the next island and slowed it, aiming for the sandy beach. Maybe if they avoided the trees, the plane wouldn't break apart.

"Put your head between your knees," he said as he looked at Harley. She'd buckled in and done it without being asked.

He pulled hard on the controls to keep the nose up as the plane descended. It bounced hard as it brushed the top of a tree. Metal screeched as the tail dragged along the treetops. His chest tightened as he heard a crunch of metal and the back of the plane pulled off.

There was no time to dwell on that. He put his full

attention on controlling the plane. His muscles burned as he fought to keep the nose from hitting the sand and crushing them. After what felt like forever, the plane jerked to a stop like it'd hit a wall. Stars exploded behind his eyes for a heartbeat before darkness enveloped him.

CHAPTER 4

Harley groaned and opened her eyes. It took a few blinks, but slowly her vision cleared. One minute she was putting her head between her legs, and the next, she was wondering what clobbered her. She had no idea how long she'd been out, either.

As she looked around, she noticed that the plane was tilted and nearly lying on its side. Ocean water smacked against her dangling legs. Suddenly, she was wide awake. She didn't know how she knew, but she knew the tide was coming in and the plane was filling with water.

A cough drew her attention to Zach, who was slumped against the cabin wall. Water splashed over his face, and she watched in horror as he remained unconscious. She might not like him, but that didn't mean she wanted him to drown. Their kiss flashed through her mind. Okay, yeah, she kissed him, but that was just an I'm-gonna-die-so-I-may-as-well-kiss-the-hot-guy type of kiss, nothing special. Why not? She didn't know if they'd survive. She still didn't know.

She quickly unbuckled her seatbelt and dropped out of the chair, careful not to land on top of him. Taking his face in her hands, she said, "Zach."

When she pulled her hand away, blood covered it. She turned his head, and a cut ran from his hairline to his eyebrow. A head injury wasn't good. "Hey, Zach, you need to wake up."

A soft moan answered her. He wasn't going to be any help.

She needed to hustle if she was getting them out of the plane. She released his buckle, and Zach fell further into the water. She hooked her arms under his armpits and pulled him free of his chair. He was all muscle and heavy.

Her gaze roamed the back of the plane, or what was left of it. If she'd stayed in her seat in the back of the plane, she'd be dead. At least half of it was sheared off, and the water was no less than waist-deep the further back she looked.

With her arm securely around his neck, she pushed off into the deeper water, working to keep them both from drowning. In the movies, he'd be carrying her out of the plane with a shadow effect behind him and an announcer talking in a deep voice saying, "In a world..." Instead, here she was, lumbering to keep them afloat.

Continuing through the plane, she could see furniture and seat cushions floating. She grabbed one and pushed it under his head to make it easier to keep him afloat. Oxygen masks swung like necklace pendants. By the time she cleared the craft, the water was chest deep. Now that they were free, the tide was pushing them toward the beach, and she was grateful.

When she hit the shore, she took Zach by the armpits again and pulled him until she was sure the water couldn't reach them. She collapsed next to him and rolled onto her back, her chest heaving.

It felt like she'd participated in a triathlon. Slowly, her racing heart returned to normal, as well as her breathing. Dark clouds swirled above, but as she lifted her head, she could see blue sky. They were on the backside of the storm now, which would have given her comfort if they weren't stranded.

She rolled onto her knees and leaned over Zach. If

she could get him halfway coherent, maybe they could get further inland so she could look for water. That was the first order of business. All those weekends camping with her grandma were going to come in handy.

"Zach." She put her fingers through a hole in her skirt and ripped a piece off, touching it to his head. The cut wasn't big, but he'd sure have a headache. "Zach, you need to wake up."

His eyes opened, and he coughed then squinted. "My head hurts."

"Yeah, I bet it does. Do you think you can stand?" Her tone was sharp and detached. She needed it to be. The kiss didn't change the situation. She didn't want to be stuck with the guy. Yeah, she'd pulled him out of the plane, but that didn't mean her attitude had changed. He was still friends with Samuel. Nothing about him had changed.

"What happened?"

"We crashed. Come on, let me help you up," she said and put her arms around his shoulders.

Zach grunted as he sat up. His head dropped to her shoulder, and he murmured, "Could I…could I sit here a second? My head's spinning, and my chest hurts." He coughed hard.

"Sure."

They sat there quietly with the sound of the surf hitting the sand. If this was a populated island and she was in her swimsuit and sipping something fruity, it'd be amazing. The water was so clear it seemed more like a painting than real life.

Zach gripped her shoulders and leaned back. His eyes still seemed unfocused. "Are you okay?"

"I'm fine. A little tired from rescuing you." She smiled.

"Good." He winced and touched his head. "I think I hit my head."

"Yeah, you did." She touched his right temple, and he sucked in a sharp breath. Maybe he'd hit his head hard enough he wouldn't remember the final moments of their crash landing. She could only hope.

"You said you rescued me?"

"You were out cold when I woke up and the water was rising. I pulled you out."

He hesitated a second, and then he buried his face in her neck as he hugged her. "Thank you," he said softly.

"It's okay." She patted his back. When he kept his hold on her, she wrapped her arms around him. Great. He was being nice. She didn't want him to be nice.

Her grandma's voice flitted in her head. *No one's an*

enemy when you're stranded. That's what she got for having a survivalist for a grandma.

Whatever issues she had with him earlier would have to be put aside, especially if they were stuck with each other. It'd take them working together to survive until they were rescued. "Really. It's okay."

His breathing sounded off, but she'd just pulled him onto the beach. Her own breathing sounded off.

"I'm sorry for offending you earlier. It's hard to trust people. I always have to be on guard. The only value I have is my money, and I don't even want it," he said.

The words were like rocks, and she was standing in a glass house. Had she judged him the way people had judged her? She'd never considered that before: someone with money not wanting that money. Samuel was cocky and confident. He loved his money. Most of the time, their conversations revolved around him taking over his father's business. "I guess it would be hard."

Zach pulled back. "My head's still spinning, but I think I can stand." With her help, he stood and wobbled.

He began coughing and didn't stop. His face turned red, and he looked pained. He pulled her down as he dropped to one knee, holding his stomach with one hand and bracing his other against the sand.

"Oh, this is bad. You need to cough the water up."

"Water?" he wheezed.

"Yeah, I don't know how much you breathed in before I woke up. If you've got water in your lungs, you could get pneumonia."

A second round of coughing hit him. Harley stood behind him with her arm around his chest, patting him on the back. "Keep trying to get it out."

A little water poured out of his mouth, and he choked. He moaned and pitched forward onto his side with Harley landing on him with a grunt.

She kneeled next to him. "No, you need to sit up."

"I can't."

Her gut said he needed to be sitting up. She had no idea why the feeling was so strong, but it was, and the last time she'd ignored her gut, she'd been dumped. "Come on," she said, putting her arms around his chest and sitting him up.

His eyes locked with hers for a brief moment, and he fell forward against her. "I'm sorry," he whispered. With the way he sounded, she suspected it was as loud as he could speak.

Why did he have to sound so sincere? "It's okay. We'll sit here until you're able to stand."

Gradually, he stopped wheezing, and it sounded like he was breathing somewhat normally. He leaned back. "I think I'm okay now."

"All right. Let's see if we can find water." That was the most important thing. Her grandma had stressed that more times than Harley could remember.

She helped him stand, put her arm around his waist, and pulled his arm across her shoulder. They walked until the sand turned to grass, and she leaned him against a tree. "You stay here. I'm going to find water, okay?"

"I'll go with you."

What did she do? It'd be faster without him, but she didn't really want to leave him. He still looked dazed. She had no idea how hard he'd hit his head. What if he fell asleep and slipped into a coma?

He leaned his back against the tree and closed his eyes, pressing his palm against his chest. "You know what? I think I'll stay here."

She chewed her thumb as she debated. He could stay. It'd be fine. "I'll try to be quick. Try not to go to sleep, okay?"

"No promises. My head hurts so bad I can hardly see, and I'm really tired."

Oh great. There was no way she could leave him

now. "Maybe staying isn't a good idea. Why don't you come with me?"

"Okay."

THE VEGETATION GREW THICKER the further into the forest they walked, and they hadn't walked that far. Harley kept her arm around his waist, even after he'd assured her he could walk, and she was probably right to keep it there. He was stumbling more than he was actually walking.

"I hope there's water close. I don't want to be that far from the beach. If someone is looking for us, I don't want them to see that wreckage and assume we didn't make it," Harley said.

He nodded and regretted it. His head still felt rattled. "Me too, but for different reasons."

She stopped walking and faced him. "Do you need to rest a second?"

"Maybe just a second." He walked a few steps and leaned his shoulder against a tree.

Harley took his face in her hands. "Look at me."

Zach locked eyes with her. "I guess I should have stayed back there."

Her eyes darted back and forth like she was

analyzing him. "No. I need to keep an eye on you. A head injury can be serious." She dropped her hands to her sides.

He wanted to argue with her, but he couldn't. His brain felt scrambled. "I'm sorry I got you into this mess. If I'd just taken a second—"

"You might still be in that plane because a *male* assistant would have been too weak to pull you out." She smiled.

A chuckle drifted from him. "True."

"You think you can walk some more. We need water."

Harley had saved his life. He didn't know how he knew it, but he did. He nodded and pushed off the tree. "Yeah, I think so."

What he wanted was to close his eyes for a minute. Maybe it would ease the thundering headache that throbbed behind his eyes. She put her arm around his waist as he put his arm across her shoulder.

"Oh, hey, there's water just a bit further!" She glanced over her shoulder toward the way they'd come. "And it's not that far."

They walked a few more feet, and Zach sat down hard on the edge of a large body of water. "I hope it's fresh water."

"Me too." Harley dipped her finger in and stuck it

in her mouth. "Cold, fresh water. It must be fed by a spring or something."

Zach lay back against the grass, and his eyes slid shut. "I just need to rest my eyes a second."

"Oh, no." Harley was next to him in a flash. Her arms wrapped around his chest and pulled him into a sitting position. "You need water too, and you need to stay awake a little longer."

"Now that you say that, I am thirsty."

She took his chin in her fingers. "Don't lie back down. I'll be right back."

"Okay."

What felt like a few seconds later, Harley kneeled facing him. "Take little sips, okay? I can only imagine how worse your head will feel if you get choked and have to cough again."

She put a large green leaf to his lips and tipped it up. Cold water dripped into his mouth. He hadn't realized just how thirsty he was until those first few drops hit his tongue. Part of him wanted to gulp the rest of it down, but the other part was smart enough to listen to the nice lady who'd rescued him. When the leaf was empty, she set it down.

"Thank you," he said. His gaze dipped to his jeans. "I'm soaked."

"We both are. The plane was filling with water, remember?"

"Oh, right."

She straightened her shoulders and looked around. "This works. The water is close and easily accessible. If I can find some dry wood, I can get a fire going. I might even be able to catch a few fish."

"How do you know how to do all this stuff?" He had no idea if he'd remember the answer.

Her lips spread into a grin. "My grandma loved camping. I went camping with her from the time I could walk until I was almost sixteen. She taught me all there is to know about survival."

"Guess I'm lucky there was a mix-up."

She lifted an eyebrow. "Never underestimate me."

"No, I don't think I will."

He put his head in his hands and exhaled. "I just need my head to stop hurting. I feel like I've been kicked."

She tipped his chin up and locked eyes with him. "Well, they aren't as dull as they were," she said and let him go. "Let me get a camp set up, and you can rest."

"I should be helping you."

"You're injured. There's no shame in that. You did pick a great island to be stranded on. So, there's that."

He chuckled. "I don't think picked is the right word."

"We'll go with that anyway. Ready to go?"

"Sure." Zach stood and stumbled, so Harley wrapped her arms around his waist and steadied him. "I feel dizzy."

She smiled. "It's okay. I'm right here." She paused a moment. "Are you ready?"

"Yeah." He stared at her and had a feeling he'd be thanking her a lot more before they were found.

CHAPTER 5

It took Harley a couple of hours, but she found what she thought was a good spot on the edge of the beach to make camp until they were found. For now, she'd gather firewood and find food. Tomorrow, she'd get a shelter built. She'd need help with the heaving lifting, and she hoped Zach would be up to the task by then.

She left him at the spot she'd picked while she gathered firewood, but she found herself hurrying so she could get back. She may not like him, but she also didn't want anything to happen to him. Being stuck on the island alone would be worse.

He'd hugged her so tightly earlier. It made her feel weird. Not as weird as the kiss was making her feel, but to her relief, he'd not mentioned that when he hugged her. And the sorrow in his voice as he spoke about people using him…that wasn't like Samuel at all. Samuel had never held her like that either. Like she was something precious and worth holding onto.

Harley shook her head to clear her thoughts. Survival mode was what she needed to be in, not… introspective *is the rich guy actually nice* mode. She reached down and picked up a piece of wood. It looked like it'd been broken during the storm. It wasn't soaking wet, and if she could break it a little more, maybe she'd find a dry center so she could cook some fish.

Something silver glinted a few feet away, and she narrowed her eyes. "A suitcase?" She dumped the wood and sprinted to the piece of luggage. It was Zach's. What were the chances hers was nearby? She lifted on her tiptoes as she scanned the area. "Chances are slim, Jim."

Well, at least he'd have something else to wear. She pulled the handle on the suitcase, and it bounced behind her as she dragged it. Stopping at the pile of wood, she stacked it against the handle and then tied it with the luggage strap to keep it in place.

It took effort and muscles she didn't know she had, but she managed to get it back to camp. "Hey—" she said and stopped abruptly.

Zach was slumped back against a tree with his chin on his chest.

She stopped fighting with the luggage and walked to him. "Zach," she said as she kneeled next to him.

He didn't so much as flinch.

"You're out aren't you?" She sighed and continued her one-sided conversation. "Your head and neck are going to hurt if I let you stay like that." Since when did she feel obligated to take care of him? So what if he had a sore neck.

Harley blew out a puff of air. She couldn't leave him like that. She hugged him around the chest and eased him back onto the ground, careful not to let his head hit the sand too hard. Still not a peep from him. Hopefully, his head injury wasn't serious.

She took a moment and studied his face. He sure was good-looking. And those lashes? Did men get extensions? They were the longest she'd ever seen on a man. Of course, he'd have killer lashes to go with those gorgeous, piercing blue eyes.

His face was so pale. He'd really been hurt, and so far, he hadn't been the jerk she needed and wanted him to be.

She brushed the back of her hand along his cheek, and her skin tingled, just as much as her lips had when she kissed him. The sensation made her jerk her hand away. What was she doing? He was a billionaire. He could be the best-looking man on the face of the planet, and she wouldn't be interested. Not in the least.

Bracing her hands on her thighs, she pushed herself up and stood. She had things to do other than drool over an unconscious man.

Her only goal was to survive. This was a bus, she was Annie, and she needed to keep the speed over fifty. What did Keanu Reeves say? Relationships based on intense situations never worked. Exactly. Why was she even thinking about it, anyway?

With an exasperated sigh, she walked to his suitcase and untied the wood. Once she had the wood stacked for the fire she'd need later, she stuck a few pieces of it into the sand where the sun could shine on them to dry their clothes.

Should she open his suitcase? If the contents were waterlogged, wouldn't he want them dried out? Plus, she needed her clothes dried too. Maybe he'd have a t-shirt she could borrow. Would he mind her borrowing it?

Harley chewed her thumb and debated a few minutes more before throwing her hands up. "If he gets mad, he gets mad. We're stranded. What's he gonna do? Banish me from the island?"

She unzipped the bag, and to her surprise, everything was dry. "Waterproof luggage?" she asked as she glanced at him over her shoulder. "Smart move."

She dug through it and pulled out a shirt. With another glance to make sure he was still asleep, she quickly undressed and pulled the dry shirt over her head. It wasn't until she had it on that she realized she was a little cold.

Was Zach cold too? Should she get his wet clothes off? She should have remembered to ask him about that before she went searching for firewood. If nothing else, his shoes had to come off before she did anything else. Waterlogged feet could quickly develop sores, and they didn't need that.

She could almost hear her grandma chastising her for leaving them on this long. It hadn't occurred to her because she'd lost her shoes in the crash.

She returned to him and pulled off his shoes and socks. "How mad will you be if you wake up with no pants on?"

With a huff, she said a quick prayer that he was wearing boxers and worked on taking his jeans off. He'd just have to keep his shirt on for the moment. Lifting him took work, and she needed to find them some food. When she finally managed to get them off, she hung them to dry. Hopefully, that would ease the awkwardness when he woke up, because she could offer a reason as to why.

Harley shielded her eyes with her hand as she scanned the horizon. The sun was setting, and she didn't want to be swimming at night. At least, not alone. She picked up the rock she'd found earlier and whittled the end of a tree limb down until she was sure it was pointy enough to spear fish.

After she was done, she set off toward the ocean. "At least the water's clear. I won't get eaten without seeing it coming." It was also a problem. The fish could see her coming too. It was going to take a lot of patience to get enough fish to feed them.

Maybe she could find a tidepool. She wasn't sure how long it'd been, but it already seemed like the tide was changing again. Hopefully, it wouldn't take too long. Her stomach was already growling.

SOMETHING INCREDIBLE-SMELLING PULLED at Zach's nose. He sat up, rubbing his eyes. As his vision cleared, he could see the sun on its way down.

Harley smiled. "Hey, you're up just in time."

"How long was I out?" His gaze dropped to his pants, or the lack thereof. "And why am I in my boxers?" He lifted his gaze to her. "And is that my shirt?"

She chuckled. "I guess you're feeling better. To the first question, I don't know. A while. I left to find firewood, and when I came back, you were out cold. Your jeans were soaked, and I took them off so they could dry. And yes, this is your shirt because your suitcase is the only one I found."

She'd gone through his suitcase, taken his pants off, and she was wearing his shirt. For a brief second, he was agitated, until it came back to him that she'd taken care of him. If it wasn't for her, he might not even be alive. He looked around the small campsite she'd picked. A fire was burning with several fish roasting over the top of it.

"I'm sorry I went through your things. I made sure to keep my focus on the clothes, and as soon as mine are dry again, I'll give your shirt back." She stood, and those incredibly long legs looked even longer, now that she was wearing his shirt that didn't even come mid-thigh.

"I—"

Harley kneeled next to him and held his face in her hands. "Your eyes are clear. At least I won't have to keep an overnight vigil."

He was okay until she touched him. Now, his

senses were on overload, and his heart pounded in his chest. "Uh." Then the kiss she'd laid on him came back in full color. How was he going to navigate that? Pretend he'd been knocked on the head so hard he didn't remember it?

"Here are your swim trunks," she said and handed them to him. He hadn't even noticed she was carrying them. Now he wished he'd brought sweatpants for her to wear.

"Thanks."

She dropped her hands. "Are you hungry?"

He cleared his throat and quickly slipped his trunks on. "Yeah." Yep, he was pretending that kiss didn't happen. As wonky as he was feeling at the moment, bringing it up would only make things worse.

"Me too." She scooted along the ground and sat with her legs curled under her. "I don't know if it's enough to fill us all the way up, but it should help."

"You got a fire going and caught fish?" He maneuvered himself until he was next to her.

She shrugged. "Yeah, why?"

"I'm kind of in awe."

Her laughter filled the air. "Does that mean you don't want to send me home the moment we get to Jamaica?"

"Uh, I think that trip has been put on hold."

"I was teasing." She bumped him with her shoulder. "Won't rescue people be able to use the little black box?"

"Well, it's not black; it's orange. And it took search teams two years to find Air France 447's black boxes, so…"

Her eyebrows lifted. "Oh, well, okay."

"Sorry."

She shrugged. "It is what it is. Guess it's a good thing I picked this spot with the fallen tree to build a shelter tomorrow."

He knitted his eyebrows together. "Why?"

"All we'll need are some branches to make a back wall and some leaves to help if it rains."

"Oh." It was his fault they were stranded, and she was doing all this work. He raked his hand through his hair. "I'm so sorry I got us into this mess. Or, at least you. If I'd just—"

"Like I said before, if things were different, you might not be here. I'm not thrilled to be stranded, but at least you aren't dead."

Before? They'd talked? He had no memory of that. All he could recall was that she'd saved him.

She pulled a fish off the fire and handed it to him. "I want that little bugger eaten first. It took me forever to catch him, and by the end, I was going to catch him if it killed me."

He tried to hand it back to her. "Then you should eat it."

"Nah, I'm not really one to dine on the corpses of my enemies."

Zach's head fell back as he laughed. His head felt better, but that movement wasn't smart. He rubbed the back of his head. "I'll have to remember that."

She pulled another fish off the fire and picked at it. "This isn't bad."

He pulled off a huge chunk of white meat and popped it into his mouth. It was tender, flakey, and sweet. He couldn't think of a time when something tasted better. Then again, he'd never been in a position where it felt like his stomach could devour itself. "This is fantastic."

"Glad you think so."

"You've cleared an area, found firewood, and built a fire. I'd say that's pretty great. I just wish I could have helped."

"Can't help getting knocked on the head."

That was true, but it didn't help any with his guilt. He didn't know what to say, though. Other than what he'd already said. They ate in silence until all six of the fish were gone.

Zach's leg bounced. He'd never been one to be still or enjoy the quiet. No, he didn't want to date, but he did enjoy having friends over. He was always going, too. Meetings, lunches, conferences—all of them keeping him busy. "I'm not really used to sitting around, twiddling my thumbs."

"Well, I think we're both going to be pros at that before we get off this island."

He smiled. She was probably right about that. It'd take a few days before Matt or Britney realized he was missing. "Did you see where the tail of the plane went?"

She shook her head. "No, I think we flew in from the other side of the island, over the trees, and landed."

Zach looked up, and treetops were sheared off. His gaze traveled to what was left of the plane. The cockpit was below the water, and the ragged metal of the body was sticking up. He knew she'd saved his life, but seeing it put it in a whole new perspective.

Harley yawned, pulled her knees up, and laid her head on them. "I think my day has caught up to me," she said and yawned again. "I'm exhausted." Her dark hair flowed down her back as she lifted her head up and pointed her face to the sky.

How was it he was just now noticing her hair? Not just her hair, but little details he'd trained himself to purposefully ignore. Details that led to racing pulses, flirty smiles, and things he didn't want.

"I'm impressed you lasted this long. I wish I could've helped more."

Harley gave him a one-shoulder shrug. "You'll make it up to me tomorrow when I'm so sore I can't move." She lay down on her side with her head resting on her arm. "I'm too tired to move."

Her eyes slid shut, and in seconds her breathing was even.

He slid closer to her and pushed her hair over her shoulder. What an incredible woman. Pulling him out of a crashed aircraft, hauling him up the beach, finding firewood and building a fire, and then catching food. All while he did nothing. That wouldn't happen tomorrow. He'd pull his weight or die trying.

CHAPTER 6

It took a few moments for Harley to put together where she was. Her body was stiff and sore. Joints popped and cracked as she stretched, and her muscles protested. She pushed herself into a sitting position and looked over at Zach.

A small smile grew on her lips as she watched him, curled on his side with his arm under his head like a cushion. Why on earth was she smiling? He *was* cute. She couldn't deny that, and a cute guy curled up asleep was something to smile at.

The spot where he'd hit his head was showing a decent-sized bruise. She wondered if he'd still have a headache when he woke up. With as hard as he hit his head, it wouldn't surprise her.

Harley chewed her bottom lip, contemplating

whether she should wake him or not. They needed a shelter, but she knew he hadn't felt well the night before. There was a part of her that felt kinda guilty. She'd fallen asleep instead of making sure he was okay.

She looked up. It wasn't superhot yet. Once the sun was in full blaze, they'd be working in the heat. He needed to wake up so they could eat and build a shelter.

She crawled over to him and kneeled next to him. "Hey, Zach, you need to wake up."

He mumbled something and rolled onto his back. Why did he have to be so cute?

"Zach, wake up." She lightly shook him.

"I don't want to," he murmured.

She chuckled. "I didn't want to either, but we have food to catch and a shelter to build."

He pushed himself into a sitting position and rubbed his eyes, wincing as his hand grazed the cut on his head.

"You've got a terrible bruise there. Does your head still hurt?"

"No, I think it probably looks worse than it feels."

"Then you must feel like roadkill."

His laugh was warm and deep, and goosebumps rolled across her. He smiled. "I'm fine."

"Okay, well, I'm going to get breakfast, then."

"Breakfast?"

She nodded. "Yeah, I found a tidal pool yesterday. Hopefully, there'll be more today so I don't have to do any deep-sea fishing."

"Okay." They stood together, and his gaze traveled down her body and back up. "By the way, that shirt looks good on you."

Her cheeks heated, and she felt the fire blaze a trail to her ears. She still had on his shirt. The shirt that barely covered her rear end. One wrong move, and he'd be getting an eyeful. At least she was wearing underwear, and they covered her more than some of the bikinis she'd tried on. Were they really any different from swimsuit bottoms? Yes, yes, they were. "Uh, yeah, I'll get it back to you when I'm finished."

"That's okay. I can't imagine trying to survive here wearing what you had on earlier. Until we have a chance to track down your luggage, just hang on to it."

She nodded and smiled. "Thanks."

"Do you mind if I tag along?"

"No, I don't mind the company." She paused a second and then began walking. "Uh, I'm going to try the tide pool again."

He crossed his arms—his huge, muscular arms—over his chest. Not that she was looking. Did he work out? He had to. Why was she even thinking that? She was supposed to be hating him.

"Your grandma taught you survival, right?"

Good. Something other than his muscles to think about. She nodded and smiled as she thought about the times she spent with her Grandma Ellis. "Yeah, she was completely wild and unpredictable. My mom didn't get along with her as well I did. They loved each other, really, but my mom could be…irritating. I love my mom, but she's beyond organized. Which is great until you come home and can't find your cereal because she's rearranged your kitchen."

Zach chuckled. "That could be a real problem. And why do I suddenly have a craving for Cocoa Puffs?"

"Probably because you can't have any."

He cast her a glance. "Probably. I think I'll live on them when I get home."

A Heavy silence fell between them as they continued down the beach. She didn't know what to say to that. Of course they'll be found? She hoped they would, especially now that she wanted Cocoa Puffs too.

They reached the tide pool, and she climbed over the rock jutting out of the sand. "Yes!"

Zach looked down into the pool. "Cool."

"I'd hoped the ones I left would still be here. I

didn't know what the wildlife was like." She chewed her bottom lip and readied her spear. A few seconds later, she threw it. "Gotcha," she said and pulled up the still-wriggling fish and took it off the spear. "Sorry, little guy."

She couldn't say it didn't feel good to see the look on his face. He hadn't expected her to be so quick. Maybe being stuck with him would be okay, especially if she kept her head on straight. Yep, it'd be just fine. They'd be found, and they'd go their merry way.

He shot her a smile, and her stomach flipped. Gah! Her body needed to stop that nonsense.

HE'D NEVER SEEN anyone spear a fish faster than her. Then again, he'd never been stranded on an island with a spear as the only way to catch fish, either. "You're fast."

"I'm motivated." She scanned the horizon. "I think I'm going to look for crabs soon. Something different. Fish every day will get old."

He smiled. "You're amazing; you know that?" Impressed, awe, surprised. None of those words seemed adequate enough for what he felt toward Harley Wilson.

She shook her head. "No, it's just stuff my grandma taught me."

"I don't know any of this stuff. My dad would never have gone camping." That wasn't completely true. When he was a kid, his dad spent all sorts of time with him. It was just the last few years he was alive that he acted like a different person.

"Why?"

Zach sighed and sat on the rock. "We had a personality conflict. I had one and he didn't."

"That would make having a relationship difficult."

"What about your dad?" he asked.

She shrugged. "Um, he decided he didn't like being married to my mom and he didn't want a baby, so two days after I was born, he left."

"Oh, wow. I'm sorry."

"It is what it is. I had my mom and grandma."

"You're an only child?"

Harley nodded and threw her spear. When she pulled it out of the water, she had another fish. "Yeah. You?" She tugged it off and put it with the other one.

"Two sisters and two brothers."

"Wow, big family. That must make get-togethers fun."

Zach chuckled. "Actually, now that my father's

gone, they're great. When he was around, they were stiff and formal and awkward."

"Gone?"

"He died before the divorce was finalized, and he'd been so bent on making my mom miserable that he forgot to change his will. So, she got everything."

Harley smiled. "I believe that in laymen's terms, that's called karma."

Zach chuckled. "If so, he deserved a double dose."

She pinned her gaze on another fish and speared it.

His eyebrows knitted together as he looked at her. "Man, you're really good at that." And she was, too. She was absolutely amazing.

"You've already said that."

"It needed to be said again." He'd never been more impressed with someone.

She chuckled. "I want to find my luggage today, if I can. This walking around in a t-shirt is making me feel weird."

Her long legs seemed to have a spotlight on them the minute she said it. "Well, I'm a guy, and I've got no problem with it."

Harley rolled her eyes. "Whatever." She paused, looking like she was trying to find something to talk about. "So, what kind of things do you do in Houston? Like, what fun things?"

"Well, before I took over the company, I liked water skiing, hiking, and going to art exhibits." His lack of trust in people had limited his social life. He liked to tell himself he had one, but if he was honest, he spent most of his time alone. "How about you? What movies have you seen recently?"

She speared another fish and pulled it off. "Uh, well, I haven't seen anything lately."

"Why not?"

A little one-shoulder shrug. "I couldn't afford it."

"Oh."

Her shoulders sagged. "Don't feel sorry for me. I really hate that."

He opened his mouth to speak and stopped.

Harley speared another fish and held his gaze. "I… rented an apartment that I shouldn't have. It was above my means, but at the time I rented it, my income was better."

"I don't feel sorry for you. I didn't know how to respond."

"I'll let it slide this time." She sank her spear into another fish and smiled as she held it up. "I think this will cover us, don't you?"

"I think so." Zach took the spear and picked up the fish. "I don't know if I can start a fire, but I can cook."

She smiled wide, and his pulse jumped. "I'll get the fire going, then."

"Uh, maybe I can learn by watching?"

"Can't hurt," she said as they began walking back to camp.

He rubbed his knuckles along his jaw. "So, uh, were you awake when the plane crashed?"

"Um, I don't think so because all I remember is a large boom. When I woke up, the cabin was filling with water. You must have hit your head pretty hard, because the water was washing over you and you weren't waking up. Do you remember anything?"

"I remember trying to aim for the beach, but that's it."

"You woke up for a bit when I got you to the beach."

He searched his memory and came up blank. There was nothing there. "I'm sorry. I don't remember that."

"Do you remember being at the spring?"

His eyebrows knitted together. "A spring?"

"Yeah, there's a spring not too far from where I set up camp, or at least, I think it's a spring. The water's pretty cold for it not to be. Guess I should have shown you that before we went fishing." Her lips turned down, and her eyebrows pulled together like she was frustrated with herself.

A spring would be nice. Maybe they could swim from time to time to kill the boredom that was sure to come. "It's okay. You can show me later. And no, I don't remember that."

"Yeah, I'm not surprised. You were really out of it."

It made him uncomfortable to know his memory was so spotty. Were there things he was missing that she wasn't telling him? If he asked, would she tell him? Did he want to know? No, he'd let it go and hope he didn't embarrass himself.

CHAPTER 7

They continued walking down the beach, and the silence stretched again. Part of her wanted to scream because she was so frustrated. They were stuck together, and trying to have a conversation with him was awkward. She didn't have anything in common with a billionaire. What could they really talk about?

She wished she'd kept her mouth shut about not being able to afford her apartment. The way he responded, all sad, bugged her. He didn't need to be sad for her. She was taking care of herself.

The only reason she had the apartment was because Samuel didn't want any girlfriend of his living anywhere that was considered a rundown shack, even though her previous apartment was nice by most people's standards.

He'd found her a place in a wealthier area, and with it came a heftier price, which she'd been able to pay until she lost her job. There were two months left on the lease, and then she'd be moving back to Lubbock.

"So, is there a boyfriend that's going to be looking to beat me up for getting his girlfriend stranded on an island when I get back?"

She turned an icy stare toward him. So much for keeping things light. Why would he ask that? Did he know she dated Samuel, and he just wasn't telling her? "No."

"Uh, bad breakup?"

Harley stopped mid-stride as fury filled her like she was a cup. This guy was friends with Samuel, and even if she did want to tell someone, it wouldn't be him. Ever. "Look, we're stranded together, but that doesn't mean I want to be your friend or that you need to know any deep details about me. In a few days, when the rich guy comes up missing, there'll be a search party so large they could find a chimera. I doubt we'll be here for more than a night."

"Um, I was just trying to make conversation. I'm not used to it being so quiet."

She clenched her jaw. "Well, get used to it."

"Okay, but can I ask one question and get an honest answer?"

She huffed. "What?"

"What did I do to make you so angry with me?"

Good grief, did he have to stare at her like that? With those piercing blue eyes? And he looked so sincere. She needed to stay mad at him. But she couldn't. She knew he didn't know anything.

Samuel had never introduced them. Sure, she'd sent a wedding invitation to him, but that didn't mean he remembered who Samuel was marrying. Her posture softened. "Nothing. I just... I don't think we need to get too chummy. We're here, and we need to make the best of it. That's all."

"But I would like to get to know you."

She tilted her head and narrowed her eyes. "Really? Because you didn't seem all that eager on the plane." Not like she'd given him the chance, either.

"Because you bit my head off when I asked you anything."

"And because I wasn't who you thought I was."

He smiled. "In my defense, I was still underestimating you."

Harley rolled her eyes. Talk about charming. He could outdo Samuel any day. She turned to hide her smile. "Fine. No, there is no boyfriend, and I figured since I'm going back to Lubbock, starting something in Houston wouldn't be a good idea."

"That makes sense."

"I thought so. How about you?"

"No, there's no one, even though my sister is determined to set me up."

She chuckled. "And suddenly being an only child isn't such a bad thing."

He laughed with her. "Sometimes it can be challenging."

"Sounds like it," she said.

Silence settled between them as they walked back to camp. They'd gone several feet before she couldn't take it anymore. "So, tell me about your friend Matt. How did you meet him? What made you decide to give him equipment?"

He chuckled, like he was reliving a good memory. "Uh, I met him at a fundraiser hosted by the Baldwins, actually. At the time, he was just looking for donors to help him start the foundation. It was right after my father died, and I wanted to feel like I was giving back."

It took strength not to recoil from the name, but she managed it. "That's nice. How long ago was that?"

"About three years ago."

"This wasn't the first trip there?"

He shook his head. "No, actually, I like being there. There's an ease about life on that island. The people are beautiful inside and out. I love the kids. Matt's wife runs a school there."

"Did you help with that too?"

His cheeks turned pink, and it was the cutest thing. Suddenly, she wanted to make him blush a lot more. "Uh, yeah, but I did it because I wanted to. No one knows it's me doing it. I make sure they keep my name out of it."

Harley stopped in her tracks. "You do it anonymously?"

Zach lowered his gaze and nodded. "I don't even know why I told you. I've never told anyone that."

A newfound respect for Zach bloomed in her heart. Samuel would've never kept anything like that a secret. He would've stood on a rooftop and shouted it. If there wasn't a way to receive attention, Samuel had nothing to do with it. "I won't tell a soul, but I think that's the neatest thing I've ever heard."

He waved her off. "It's not a big deal. I have the money, and they needed it."

Huh. Maybe he wasn't like Samuel after all. Just because Zach knew Samuel didn't mean they were alike. But they'd only been on the island for a day. It's not like she knew him. What if he was just telling her all that stuff because it made him look good?

No, just like her gut said he needed to sit up, her gut said he was being truthful. How could she keep hating him if he was a good person? She nearly chuckled out loud. What a joke.

She'd never been able to really hate anyone, no matter how much she wanted to. Billionaire or homeless, it didn't matter. Her grandma had taught her to treat people based on who they were, not what they had.

A WEIRD FEELING settled in the pit of Zach's stomach. He wasn't sure why he told Harley about donating the money. It'd just spilled out. And then the way she'd looked at him, like she was in awe. The heat had rushed to his cheeks. He couldn't remember the last time that had happened.

At least she didn't feel like an iceberg any longer. He hadn't realized the minefield he was stepping into when he asked about her relationship status. If he'd known, he never would have asked. He wasn't even sure why he'd asked in the first place.

"Yeah, but a lot of people would give the money

because they want the accolades to go with it. You're doing it because you want to, not because you want a pat on the back. There's something to be said for that," she said.

"Uh." Now his ears were on fire.

She shot him a smile and caught her lip between her teeth. "You keep blushing like that, and we won't need a fire to cook the fish."

He laughed. "Are you always so blunt?"

"Kinda," she said and shrugged. "It didn't make me very popular with my peers."

"I can't picture you being anything other than popular."

"You can't make me blush, so don't even try."

He grinned. "I bet I can."

"Nope. I'm stone-cold."

He didn't believe that for a second, and he wondered what it would take to see her cheeks turn crimson. "I'll find a way."

"You can try, but you'll fail," she said as they reached camp.

She had a fire going and the fish cooking in no time, even though he'd offered to cook. He'd never really cared for fish, but he was finding fresh-caught fish was a completely different thing. The way she cooked it made it tender and flakey. The night before, he was hungry, so he'd figured that was why it had tasted so good. Nope, it was just as good the second time.

After they finished eating, they went to work on finding supplies for a shelter. The forest floor was so green. Birds in vibrant colors nested in trees above their heads. It would have been a great getaway if it weren't for the whole no-one-knew-where-they-were part.

"So, you know what I do," Zach said, "but you never really said what you do. I have a feeling you're more than an assistant."

Harley laughed. "Well, I was an assistant to Trixie Tanner before she fired me."

"Trixie Tanner? The party planner?" She was the go-to when it came to parties in his circle.

"Yeah, but I was dating…someone, and next thing I know, I'm fired. Once she fired me, I couldn't find anywhere that would hire me. It's been four months. That's why I'm going back to Lubbock. To hopefully start my own business there."

"You don't know why you were fired?"

She shrugged. "I have no idea. She called me into her office and said she no longer required my services. That was it. I couldn't get anything else out of her."

"And you couldn't find employment anywhere

else? Working for Trixie would have opened doors for you in other places."

"You'd think so, but that wasn't the case."

Zach nodded. Maybe he'd find out why no one would hire Harley. It was the least he could do since she saved his life. "I bet you were good at it."

"You don't know me. You can't say that."

"Yes, I can. A woman who can pull a man my size out of a crashed plane, make a fire, spear fish, and all this other stuff can most certainly plan a fantastic party."

A smile lit up her face that could've eclipsed the sun. His heart skipped a beat. It'd been so long since that happened that his stomach felt like butterflies caught in cobwebs.

Her eyes glistened, and she turned away. "Thank you," she said softly.

"I wouldn't say if it weren't true."

She nodded and remained quiet after that, but the smile never left her face. For some unknown reason, that made him practically giddy. Which made no sense. He wasn't interested in her, or anyone for that matter. He just wanted to say something nice.

The sun was low in the sky by the time they returned to camp again with enough branches that Harley was sure she could build a back wall against the fallen tree. He had no idea how she was going to do it, but he'd learned quickly that she was capable of way more than he'd ever expected. He no longer questioned or doubted her abilities.

And he was glad he didn't. She took the branches they'd gathered and began stabbing them in the dirt before leaning them against the fallen tree. In no time, she had a wall built and was using large leaves to cover it.

He couldn't say he wasn't impressed. In fact, he felt stupid ever thinking she couldn't hack an assistant's position. "I really underestimated you."

"And what have we learned?"

"To not do that again."

She grinned. "Good boy."

His mouth dropped open. "You better not pet me."

"It's not like you could catch me if I did."

"I'm faster than I look."

She lifted an eyebrow, and the corners of her mouth twitched. "Okay."

He narrowed his eyes. "Why do I get the feeling you're patronizing me?"

"I'm agreeing with you. That's all."

Zach could see her fighting not to grin. He shook his head and rolled his tongue along the inside of his cheek. "Fine."

She looked around. "I think this is the part where we become expert thumb twiddlers."

He laughed, and it came from deep in his stomach. "I haven't laughed like that in a long time."

"Glad to be of service." Harley chewed her lip and sat so she could look out over the beach.

A weird feeling tickled in his chest, and he shrugged it off. "May I sit by you?"

She lifted her gaze to his. "Sure, I don't mind."

He sat about a foot from her with his knees drawn to his chest and his arms draped across them. They sat in companionable silence as foamy waves flowed in and out. It was so rhythmic it was soothing.

"Man, it's sure pretty out here. I've never seen a sky so painted," she said, yawning as she lay back on the sand. "I shouldn't have sat down. I'm exhausted."

Zach opened his mouth to respond, but when he looked at her, she was already asleep. He slid closer to her and pushed her hair over her shoulder. He'd never met a more amazing woman.

He stood, picked her up, and carried her to the shelter she'd built. He sat down with her in his arms. When he'd met her at the hangar, there was no denying she was beautiful. There was a gracefulness about her that he'd noticed, and he worked to not notice things about women. Now, as he looked at her, she'd gone from beautiful to breathtakingly gorgeous. There was so much more to her than he could have ever guessed.

She took a deep breath and turned into him, pressing the flat of her hand against his chest. How could she look so good in an oversized t-shirt? And why did his heart race, knowing it was his shirt she was wearing? Too much had happened to be analyzing anything.

What he needed was sleep before his overactive mind got him in trouble. Tomorrow, he'd look at things objectively, and he'd be okay.

Zach laid her down and stretched out next to her, drifting to sleep while listening to the sound of Harley's breathing and the ocean hitting the shore.

CHAPTER 8

A salty breeze caressed Harley's skin as she woke up. Her body ached from the previous two days, and she went to stretch, trying to ease the ache, when she realized she was lying next to Zach. Not just lying next to him. Her arm was over his chest, and her leg was on top of his. When had she lain down in the shelter? All she remembered was falling asleep. She must have been so tired she didn't remember crawling inside.

She swallowed hard. How had she gotten herself so tangled up with him? And how was she going to untangle herself without waking him up and embarrassing herself? With as much care as she could muster, she pulled her leg off of his and lifted her arm from across his chest.

His hand traveled up her back, and he rolled to his side, facing her. Her eyes widened as his other arm wrapped around her and pulled her closer. What was she going to do now? Did she try to wiggle out of his arms like she was in a tight tunnel? Did she wake him up?

Before she could decide, his eyes opened, and he stared at her. Geez, he was good-looking. And he smelled like salt, sand, and ocean. She'd always liked the way the beach smelled. Her heart shimmied like it was high on Red Bull, and she found it hard to breathe.

"Uh," she said as heat burned her cheeks.

It was like she'd broken the trance, and he quickly let her go. "Sorry."

She scrambled away from him and grabbed the spear. "Yeah, I'm going fishing. Be back later." Then she raced down the beach and didn't stop until her feet were in the ocean.

She pressed her hand to her chest. "Okay, heart, look. We're stuck with this guy, and you can't go getting all…whatever that was back there. Remember what happened last time? The guy at the corner market knew what flavor of ice cream I liked. And remember the crying? I think I still have puffy eyes from that."

"Do you always talk to yourself?" Zach asked.

Harley squeaked. As she spun around, her feet twisted and her knees buckled. In seconds, Zach grabbed her by the arms and kept her from face-planting in the water.

"I'm sorry. I didn't mean to scare you," he said.

"Uh. Yeah, no problem." She pulled out of his grip and smiled. "Thanks."

"So, do you? Always talk to yourself?"

She squeezed her eyes shut. "How much of that did you catch?"

"Just something about puffy."

Oh, thank goodness. "Just don't want to catch the little puffy guys. They're not edible. In fact, they're poisonous."

"Right." His smile reached his eyes, and the way they twinkled made her wonder if he wasn't being entirely truthful. "Any chance I can fish today?"

"Yeah, of course." She found herself looking forward to it. Teaching him to fish would be fun. She could see him getting flustered. It wasn't as easy as it looked. When her grandma taught her, it'd taken her forever to get it.

Zach grinned like he'd won something. "Okay."

They walked down the beach, and for a reason she

didn't understand, she felt more comfortable with him now. "Have you ever spearfished before?"

"No, but I can't see it being all that hard. I have *fished* before."

She rolled her lips in. Fish were a lot quicker when there weren't hooks involved. "You think so, huh?"

"How hard can it be?"

Harley couldn't stop herself from giggling.

"You're laughing at me."

"Oh no. I wouldn't dare do such a thing."

He shot her a look that made her mouth go dry. "Maybe I'll wait. You've bruised my ego."

Mentally, she chastised herself. She was flirting with him and had no business doing so, but it sure was fun. Good grief, he had a smile that could light the sky. That olive complexion and dark hair with those eyes... He was one fine man. She could see his gorgeous self trying his hand at spearing fish and failing so badly. It'd be fun to laugh at him.

As they neared the tide pool, she handed him the spear. "There you go."

"You aren't going to give me tips?"

"Nope. You do things your way."

Zach eyed her and then stepped into the pool. He held up the spear, took aim, and threw it. After a few more tries, he'd cursed under his breath so many times the sun was blushing.

For Harley, it was the best entertainment she'd ever had, and even better, it was free. She laughed so hard her stomach hurt.

"Fine. I'm hungry, and I give up for now." He stepped out of the pool and shoved the spear into her hand.

It took her a minute to stop laughing, but once she did, she quickly caught breakfast. "It's harder than it looks."

"Yeah, I got that."

She giggled again as he picked up the fish she'd caught. They walked back to camp, and he didn't ask to be taught how to make fire, which didn't surprise her. It shouldn't have, because he was still grumbling about not be able to catch anything.

The angrier he got, the cuter he was. The thought smacked her. Okay, yes, he was cute, but she wasn't interested. One morning of flirting and laughing didn't change anything. She wasn't falling for another rich guy, no matter how adorable he was.

AFTER THEIR MEAL, Harley wanted to see if she could

find her luggage. Of course, Zach offered to tag along. Other than it was something to do, he wanted to feel useful after everything she'd done. His hope was that he was the one who found her luggage. Aside from hoping to feel better about himself, he liked seeing her smile.

The foliage made it difficult to find things. Zach watched Harley as she walked ahead of him, her long legs gliding over calf-high bushes. He needed to find that luggage before his brain turned to mush from seeing her in that t-shirt.

"I'm not seeing anything. Who knows where it could be. I'm sorry I'm going to need your shirt a little longer."

His heart nearly skipped with glee. "That's okay." His head screamed *no* like Rocky screamed *Stella*.

"I wanted to go swimming."

"Well, I have more than one t-shirt in my suitcase."

She turned, and his breath caught. This amazing woman was wearing his shirt, looking like she could be featured in a fashion magazine, and she wore the most innocent look on her face, like she had no idea the effect she was having.

"You wouldn't mind?"

"Uh, yeah. I mean, no, of course not." He needed to get it together.

She tilted her head and gave him a smile so spectacular that it may as well have had a chorus of angels backing it up. "Thanks."

He cleared his throat. "You're welcome."

They walked back to camp and grabbed a dry t-shirt before going to the spring. The entire way, Zach wondered how he was going to swim with her and keep his head clear. He had rules. Reasons. And a bunch of other garbage he couldn't remember as to why he shouldn't be—wouldn't be—interested.

She dipped her toe in and yanked it back. "I know I can wade in here, but I think my strategy should be to just go for it."

Zach hung back, debating what he should do. He wanted to swim. It was hot, and the water looked inviting. But it wasn't the water causing his hesitation.

"You're swimming too, right?"

He lifted his gaze to hers. Amber eyes? Why didn't he notice that before? Maybe it was the sun. That was it. It was the light. "Uh."

"Please? It's no fun to swim alone."

Nope. "Yeah, I'm swimming." What happened? How did nope turn to yeah between his brain and his mouth? It wasn't that far of a distance.

A wide smile spread on her lips. "This'll be fun." She looked over the edge of the water. "It's pretty clear, and I don't see anything that could hurt us. I think I'll just fall in. Just in case." She put her back to the water, held her nose, and let herself fall. When her head broke the water, she gasped.

"Is it freezing?"

"It's a shock at first, but it's not too bad."

Zach needed to cool down anyway. He followed Harley's lead and let himself fall back. The water closed around him, knocking the wind out of him. Either his body was way overheated, or the water was colder than he was led to believe.

He fought to reach the surface and sucked in a lungful of air as he hit the surface. "You lied!"

"I didn't. It's not so bad when you get used to it."

Zach swam closer to her. "I don't think I've ever been in water this cold."

"I don't think it's that cold. I think we were that hot."

She had that last part right. In more ways than one. "If you say so."

Harley laughed and flicked him with water.

"I'll have you know, I'm a champion water splasher!"

She gave him a one-shoulder shrug. "At this point, you're all talk." She flicked him again.

"Oh, it's on." Zach skated his hand over the surface

of the water and splashed her. From there, they traded splash after splash.

Finally, Harley held her hands up and sputtered after being hit. "Okay, I'm done."

Zach took a deep breath, thankful the war was over. "And what do we say?"

She floated a second, seeming to catch her breath, and said, "You're a sucker." She smacked him in the face with water and quickly swam away.

He rubbed his hands down his face, wiping the water off. "I'm coming for you. Just so you know."

She threw her head back and laughed. "I'm faster than you."

Zach plowed through the water toward her.

Her eyes went wide. "Okay, I was just kidding."

He didn't answer and kept swimming for her. With the right motivation, he wasn't all that slow. She squealed as he caught her around the waist. "I've gotcha now." Her back was pressed against his stomach, and he pinned her arms to her chest as he laughed.

She craned her neck and looked at him. "The water's not so cold now, is it?"

His smile faltered. Her eyes held his, and he swallowed hard. She was too close, and now he had clear sight of her lips. Perfect, full, deep-rose, and the most kissable he'd ever seen.

"See? A little playing, and it's perfect." She grinned.

He let her go and moved back. "Yeah, it's great."

"I'm thinking we head back to camp and relax for a while before we have to hunt down more food."

Zach nodded because he wasn't sure he could get his tongue to work again. He had rules, and for some crazy reason, he was having trouble remembering them when she was around. Why were they so hard to recall?

The logical part of his brain said it was because she saved his life and they were stranded together. That she was a beautiful woman and any man would feel what he was feeling. The other not-so-logical part said it was because of her. There was something different about her. He felt like an invisible string was wrapping around him and pulling him to her.

The internal war made his head hurt. She'd saved his life. That would be enough to cause all sorts of weird feelings. That had to be it. He was Zachary Wolf. He didn't get involved with anyone. Not even Harley Wilson, no matter how incredible she was.

CHAPTER 9

"If it weren't for the fact that we're stranded, this would be a lovely vacation," Harley said as she dug her toes into the sand.

After swimming in the spring, she and Zach had returned to camp and decided to limit their activity so they didn't overheat. They were finding the midday sun on their tropical oasis to be blisteringly hot.

Zach chuckled. He was stretched out next to her in the shade, watching the ocean roll in and out. "No, this isn't too bad. It would be better if we had drinks with little umbrellas."

"Yeah, that would be nice. Something fruity and cold."

"I think I might dream about it tonight."

Harley nodded. "Yeah, that and Cocoa Puffs."

"And drinking the chocolate milk after."

"Cold chocolate milk."

Zach held up his hand. "Stop. This is getting torturous."

She laughed. "Wimp."

He glanced at her. "I'm not a wimp. I just know my limits."

"Your limits make you sound wimpy."

"You're not funny."

She rolled her lips in to hide her smile.

"And I can see you trying to not smile."

Harley busted out laughing. "I was saving your wimpy feelings." He was so fun to tease, with the incredulous look on his face and the way his cheeks would turn pink. Even better when his jaw would drop. It was hysterical.

He huffed and rolled, facing away from her. "You're mean."

"Oh, come on. I'm teasing."

"No. You hurt my feelings this time."

She sat up. "Are you messing with me?"

"Leave me alone."

Her mouth fell open. Had she really hurt his feelings? That's not what she was trying to do. All she wanted to do was make him laugh because she liked his laugh. She leaned over him and cupped his cheek, forcing him to look at her. "Zach, I'm so sorry. I wasn't trying to—"

A huge smile grew on his lips. He snaked his hands out and grabbed her by the waist, pulling her over him, and then began tickling her.

"Oh, you faker. You don't play fair!" She laughed and squealed. "Stop!"

His fingers were running up and down her ribs and stomach like they were on speed. "Nope. It's time to teach you a lesson about being nice." He continued to tickle her until tears streamed from her eyes.

"I'm sorry. Stop!" The words came out in puffs as she tried to catch her breath.

He slowed his assault but didn't stop. "Are you going to be nice?"

"Yes, I'll be nice." She choked out.

"Thank you," he said and rolled onto his back.

"That was not fair at all. I was just teasing."

Zach lifted an eyebrow. "You have your way, and I have mine."

She smacked him in the chest with the back of her hand. "Tickling me wasn't fair."

Quicker than she would've given him credit for, he rolled onto his side and grabbed her wrists, pinning them above her head. "I'm not afraid to tickle you again." His eyes nearly twinkled.

Her eyes widened. "No!"

"Then. Be. Nice."

"What's your definition of nice?" she asked, teasing him a little more.

He held her gaze, and her heart thundered in her chest. "Not picking on me."

Harley took a deep breath and still felt dizzy from lack of oxygen. "You do realize my choice of entertainment is limited."

"And I'm not for entertainment."

Clearly, he didn't understand how wrong he was. "I was having a great time."

"Do I need to tickle you?"

"I thought we were talking. I haven't been mean."

"You're borderline, and since I'm judge and jury, that's my call."

She lifted her head off the sand and narrowed her eyes. "Talk about not fair." It was a mistake. His lips were so close, and they looked so soft. Suddenly, nothing was funny. She needed to get away from him. All these weird thoughts and funny, jiggly feelings. He was no different from Samuel. Rich, elite, and on this island, he could use her up until there was nothing left. She let her head drop back on the sand. "Could you let me go, please?"

He dropped his hands from her wrists. "I—"

She scrambled away and stood. "I need to go for a walk."

Harley didn't wait for an answer. She just ran like her life depended on it. She didn't stop until her lungs begged for mercy. Her knees hit the sand as tears trickled down her cheeks.

How close had she been to forgetting who and what that man was? A great smile and a nice laugh. Was she that easy? She'd never felt so cheap in her life until that moment.

That thought hit her so hard it knocked her back on her heels. She palmed her chest and curled into a ball. Had she been that easy for Samuel too? Was she that kind of girl? The one guys saw as a simple target to use and throw away?

This was only the third day. Why was it so easy to forget everything when she was around him? Why was she so weak? Could she be that desperate to be wanted that she'd take whatever was thrown her way?

She didn't want to be, but maybe she was. Was it so wrong to want to be loved? No, it wasn't. She just needed higher standards. One a billionaire couldn't reach standing on his tiptoes.

It felt like hours had passed since Harley left. The sun had been high in the sky, and now it was starting to hit the treetops.

Zach scrubbed his face with his hands. He'd only been playing. The same thing Harley was doing. He hadn't meant to upset her, but their moment of playfulness had turned serious before he knew what hit him.

One minute they were laughing and teasing one another, and the next, her lips were so close that the temptation to close the gap was almost more than he could fight. It'd felt like someone pushing him into her.

Her eyes had turned stormy, her voice had cracked, and the moment she was free of him, it was a blaze of legs and t-shirt as she raced down the beach away from him.

How much worse would it have been had he kissed her? Zach sighed in frustration and punched the sand with his fist. Whatever. He needed to keep his distance from now on. No more touching or teasing or anything. They were stuck together, and as soon as they were rescued, they'd go back to their lives —separately.

He squeezed his eyes shut and tried to mentally

steel himself so that when she returned, he could handle being near her.

"Hi."

His eyes snapped open, and there she stood, tall and beautiful. The breeze was playing with her hair, and strands were floating across her face. His chest tightened. Where had his pep talk gone? "Are you okay?"

"I'm fine. I just needed a second." She held up her hand. "I know you said you wanted to learn to fish, but I went ahead and got food. I figured since I was gone so long that I'd—"

"It's okay," he said and shrugged. "Can you teach me how to make a fire?"

"Sure."

She set the fish down and arranged the firewood with a little bit of bark tinder in the middle. "You need to make sure there's enough space for air to feed it."

"Okay."

"This is called the bow and drill method."

Zach paid close attention to everything she said, from the groove in the wood to how to use the spindle. When it was his turn, she was more patient than he could have ever been. After the hundredth try, he threw his hands up and exhaled. "I'm never getting this."

"Sure, you are. It takes practice. You think because you have a hairy chest that it should be some innate, manly talent?"

"Yes."

She laughed. "That's not how it works."

Zach groaned. "Fine." He tried again and failed. "The fish will rot before I get a fire started."

"No, it won't. Here." She pressed herself against his back and held his hands. Her breath tickled his ear, and his pulse raced. "Okay, you have to be consistent. It's the friction that creates the fire." She covered his hand with hers and guided it as he held the spindle, moving it steadily up and down, and in seconds, the tinder was smoking. "See. You can do it."

He smiled at the accomplishment, or, well, part of the accomplishment, since he'd had help getting it started.

Harley leaned away from him. "Now, cup it and blow gently on it to stoke the ember."

Zach did exactly what she said, and a small flame flickered. "Yes!" He punched the air with his fist. "Yes!"

She smiled. "I knew you could do it."

He returned her smile and held her gaze. She was amazing. "My family would love you. You're incredible."

She pulled her gaze from his and lowered it. "I doubt that."

"Why would you say that? You're unbelievable. You have this grace about you. You're patient. I could've drowned, and you pulled me out. You built this camp by yourself. You are amazing."

"I've been around...people like you. They made sure I knew I wasn't good enough. The only reason you're saying those things is because you're stuck with me. As soon as we're off this island, you won't even remember my name."

He felt like he'd been punched. Anger burned in the pit of his stomach. "You don't know me or my family. What about me has given you even a hint that I'd be like that?"

"Have you forgotten our conversation on the plane? When you were going to send me home because I wasn't good enough? Anyway, you didn't have to do anything. You're friends with—" She froze and clamped her lips shut. "I think you've proven you can cook, and I'm no longer hungry." She turned on her heels and crawled into the shelter, curling into a ball with her back to him.

He clenched his jaw. Fine. If that's how she wanted to be, then that's how it'd be. It felt like actual fumes were pouring out his ears. What right did she have to accuse him or his family of being snobby jerks? She didn't know him or his family. His father had died long before she arrived in Houston, so surely she didn't know about his reputation. And if she'd worked parties with Trixie Tanner, then she'd know his family was nothing like his father. And Zach hadn't meant anything against her worth on the plane.

He stewed a second longer.

Before he could stop himself, he stalked to the shelter and crawled in. "There are two sides to this, and you don't just get to decide when the conversation is over."

"Leave me alone."

"No. You accused me of something that's blatantly false, and I already told you I was underestimating you on the plane. I was upset about the situation. It was nothing personal about you." He paused. "And friends with who?"

Harley pulled herself tighter and remained quiet.

Zach touched her arm. "It's not fair to accuse me of something and then walk away mad. I should get to defend myself."

She whipped around and glared at him. "I have every right to be mad. People like you, people with money, you don't care how you treat people like me. I'm just some *thing* that's useful for the moment, and when you're done with me, it'll be over. You'll throw me away, and that'll be it."

"This is nuts, Harley. What have I done to make you think that?"

"It doesn't matter. Leave me alone."

Zach couldn't wrap his mind around what had happened. Why was she so angry with him all of a sudden? "Could you, at least, tell me what I did wrong?"

She lay down with her back to him. "Please don't make me talk to you right now. I'm mad, and I know you've been hurt before. I don't want to hurt you like I've been hurt." Her body shook, and soft sobs poured from her.

What did he do? Who had hurt her so badly that she'd break down like this? Zach lay down behind her and wrapped his arms around her, pulling her back tightly against his chest. Part of him wanted to offer words of comfort, but what did he say? Would they comfort or just cause more grief? He'd learned from his mom that sometimes the best comfort was silence and an embrace that made you feel safe. After everything she'd done for him, that was the least he could do.

CHAPTER 10

Harley teetered on the edge of being fully awake. Her dreams had been a torrent of emotions and images. In the last one, Samuel hadn't left her at the altar. They were married, and from all appearances, she was living an incredible life with him in their amazing home. Everything was beautiful. He loved and cherished her, but when they entered the door of their house, it was dark and decaying.

It was this dream that had pulled her out of her deep sleep. The only reason she hadn't ventured outside was because of how embarrassed she was about the night before. One minute she'd been fine, and the next, she'd seen red and lost it.

Worse, she'd almost told Zach about Samuel, something she didn't want him to know. His friend had tossed her aside. What if Samuel's opinion of her held weight with Zach?

Although, Zachary Wolf was proving to be nothing like Samuel Baldwin, and if Zach wasn't like Samuel, there would be no reason to stay away from him. She needed Zach to be a snobby elitist. At least, until she was off the island—and away from him.

"I know you're awake," Zach said.

Her heart doubled its pace, and she put her back to the camp. She didn't know how to talk to him. Even if she did, what would she say? Sorry, I got really mad, freaked out, and then bawled like a baby?

She felt the air move and the warmth of his body behind her.

"Hey."

Slowly, she looked over her shoulder, and he had those incredible eyes pinned on her. "Hi," she said softly as she rolled onto her back and sat up. "I'm sorry."

He tugged her to him and wrapped his arms around her. She was tucked against him and being squeezed like he was trying to mend her. "I don't know who hurt you, but I can promise you that if I find out who it was, they'll regret it." He placed a kiss on the top of her head.

Oh, he was so warm, and he was holding her so

tightly. It was the kind of hold she'd dreamed of. The kind that said, "There's safety here. The world can't get to you." She didn't want to like it, but she couldn't fight melting into him.

"I realize we're stranded, but I'm just me. I'm not telling you anything I wouldn't tell you anywhere else. I think you're incredible, and whoever thought differently was wrong."

She had no doubt he believed that, but as soon as he found out it was his friend and his friend's family, he'd change his tune. It was nice to hear it coming from him, though, even if she knew it wouldn't last. She'd saved his life, and that was why he was being sweet to her.

"I don't know about you, but I'm starving. I think I could eat a gallon of fish and still want seconds," he said.

Harley chuckled and pulled back. "Couldn't catch 'em, huh?"

"Didn't try. I was worried about you."

She lowered her gaze. "I'm sorry."

He tipped her chin up with his finger and locked eyes with her. "I'll make a deal with you. You catch the fish, and I'll find who hurt you and beat 'em up for you."

"I don't think you'd do that."

Zach shot her a smile that made her thankful she wasn't standing. "I don't strike you as the violent type?"

"No," she said, barely above a whisper. That was as loud as she could get it. He was staring at her so intently, she couldn't breathe. "But I don't mind catching the fish." It would be nothing to lean forward and touch her lips to his. In her mind, she pictured it, and goosebumps lined her arms.

"Are you cold?"

"Uh, no."

He tilted his head. "You're shaking."

"I think it's just because I'm hungry." She almost added, "For you," but she got her wits quick enough that she didn't blurt that out. Thank goodness. He'd have thought she was super pathetic if she'd said that out loud. It was stupid to even think that way. It'd only been four days. So what if he wasn't anything like she thought.

He tugged her to him again, and his mouth moved against her ear. "I'm thankful there was a mix-up, and not just because you saved my life. I think it'd be boring if I were here with anyone else."

"Says the man who tickled me because I was mean."

Zach leaned back. "You *were* being mean."

"I was teasing. You tricked me and then tickled me

until I couldn't breathe. I'd say you're the mean one. I bet you're ticklish too."

His eyes went wide. "Don't you dare tickle me."

"Oh, I wouldn't tickle you in here. You'd break my shelter."

"I wouldn't."

"I can see it now. You flailing around, begging me to stop, and then, wham, my shelter is toast."

He shook his head and rolled his eyes. "You're not funny at all, and I'm starving. Let's get something to eat and then go swimming."

There was a possibility she'd been too quick to judge Zachary Wolf. So far, he wasn't anything like Samuel. Zach was warm, funny, sweet, and caring. When she tried to apply those qualities to Samuel, they didn't fit as well—or at all, really. Maybe being left at the altar was a blessing. Maybe she needed to look at Zach a little differently too.

THE SAND STRETCHED out before Zach as he rested in the shade. He and Harley had eaten and then gone swimming until they were exhausted and then returned to camp. Now, they were sitting in the same spot as the day before, watching puffy animal-shaped clouds drift overhead.

"I think that one looks like a dragon," Harley said.

His thoughts weren't on the clouds. No, his mind kept playing that morning over and over. He hadn't meant to hug her. He'd meant to tell her it was okay, but then she'd looked at him with those sad amber eyes. All rationale had poured out of his ears like Niagara Falls. He'd wrapped his arms around her, and every nerve ending felt like it'd been hit with electricity.

Then she'd softened against him, and he couldn't fight how right it felt to have her in his arms. And that breathy *no* as he made her look at him. It had taken more willpower than he knew he had to keep from kissing her. He knew her lips would be soft; he just knew it. But he'd kept his wits and not kissed her, despite how many times he'd wanted to kick himself for not taking the chance.

He tried to shake the thoughts and concentrate on the clouds. "A dragon? Really? It looks like a worm to me."

"Can't you see its wings? Worms don't have wings."

"I don't see wings."

She rolled on her side and faced him. "We're going to have to get your eyes checked."

"Or yours, because you're seeing things that aren't there."

"There are wings on that worm which make it a dragon."

He leveled his eyes at her. "Why do you have to be so contrary?"

"Where'd you get that word, Buffalo Bill?"

He rolled onto his side and faced her with his elbow propping him up. "You know, you acted like you didn't like me right after we took off from Houston. And now, you're picking on me nearly non-stop."

The corners of her lips twitched. "Because my choices in company are so limitless?"

Zach scoffed. "You're being mean again."

"Do *not* tickle me."

"Then stop being so mean."

She laughed. "Stop making it so easy."

He exhaled in frustration and flopped onto his back. "You're infuriating." He'd never met anyone like her. Someone who didn't treat him like they had to be careful. Those were the people who usually wanted something from him, so they'd feed his ego to get what they wanted.

Suddenly, she had her hand braced in the sand and she was leaning over him. The sun haloed her head, and the tips of her hair brushed his chest. His heart screamed *whoa*, and his head sounded alarms. "I really am teasing. I don't mean to hurt your feelings. It's just…"

He needed his tongue to work. "Just what?"

A little shrug and a nibble on her bottom lip made his pulse quicken. "It's just that I know you feel guilty about stranding us here, and I thought maybe if I made you laugh you wouldn't feel so bad. And, I like it when you smile because it makes your eyes sparkle." She bent down and kissed his cheek. "If I've hurt you, I'm truly sorry."

The tingle where she kissed him was like a pebble in a pond with the ripples of the tiny action sending a shockwave through him. "My feelings aren't hurt. I'm teasing you back."

Her lips curved up. "Are you sure? You can be honest."

"I am. Actually, I've liked it. Most people don't treat me like a regular person. They always act like they're walking on eggshells. Mostly because they want something from me."

She combed her fingers through his hair, and his breath caught. Her eyebrows knitted together as she held his gaze. "I can't even begin to imagine. People think money is the only thing that matters, but it's not. It can't hold you like you're wanted and precious.

Can't tell you you're beautiful. Definitely can't wipe your tears. It's just paper. Really, it's kind of worthless unless it's being used to do something worth remembering."

"Yeah, that's true," he said barely above a whisper.

"I'm kind of ashamed. I judged you the way I was judged. It wasn't fair. I owe you an apology because you've been nothing like the people I've met."

His heart was racing like it was a Camaro on a quarter mile. He didn't know what to say. What people? The Baldwins? He wanted so badly to ask, but he didn't want her to freeze him out. "It's okay." Actually, it was more than okay. She was the most kissable woman he'd ever met. She was hovering over, and all he needed to do was lift on his elbows and he'd be kissing her.

Harley caught her bottom lip with her teeth. "You're very—" She stopped short, and her eyes widened. "Funny."

"Why do I get the feeling that's not what you were going to say?"

"I don't know."

"What were you going to say?"

She straightened and moved just out of reach. "Weird-looking."

"I don't think that's right either. What was it?"

"You don't need to know."

His mouth dropped open. What could she have started to say that would have made her react like that? He narrowed his eyes. "You were going to say something either nice or embarrassing."

"Was not. I was going to tell you that you have a big head. I was trying not to be mean."

"Liar."

She angled herself away. "Am not."

"Then tell me what you were really going to say."

"No, because…no."

Something in her voice made him pause. "Why?"

Harley pierced him with a look. "Because I want to hate you, but I don't. I like you, and I don't want to mess it up."

"Hate me? Why?" Why would she want to hate him?

She stood abruptly. "I'm going to hunt for crabs for dinner. I'll be back later."

He gaped after her as she sprinted away. What could she have said that would have…Could she have been thinking the same thing he was? Would kissing her mess things up? He couldn't picture anything that could change how he felt about her.

His thoughts skidded to a stop. Felt about her? He didn't feel anything for her. Gratitude. Admiration.

Strength. That's what he thought. Nothing else. Then his brain turned traitor. She was beautiful, sweet, soft, and all the things he pictured as wonderful. It wasn't hard to think about a relationship when Harley was standing next to him.

As he sat up, he raked his hand through his hair. Suddenly, the island felt too small. He needed to be found sooner rather than later, or he'd be in trouble.

CHAPTER 11

*S*tupid crabs. No, it wasn't their fault Harley couldn't stop thinking about Zach or nearly saying something stupid. She'd almost told him he was kissable. She was losing her mind. And she was stuck on the stupid island for who knows how long with him. What if she slipped up and said something before they were rescued? How weird would it be?

How had she lost her grip so quickly? Just because he was being sweet and vulnerable? That was no excuse to let herself think of him as more than just a guy she was stranded with. Her anger and determination to keep herself safe needed a refill.

She stalked back to camp and stopped as he lifted his gaze to hers. Stars in the heavens, he was cute. That scruffy hair, and now he had a little stubble growing. Although, smooth-faced Zach was her favorite. Mentally, she took herself by the shoulders and gave herself a good shake to snap her out of it. She needed to put some distance between herself and his cute face.

Harley toed the sand. "I came back to tell you I'm going to go explore. Sitting around is driving me nuts."

"You too?"

Oh great. He was going to ask to tag along. How was she going to stew and be mad at him if he was right next to her?

"Well, yeah, but…"

"You wanted to go alone."

Aw, goodness. Why did he have to sound so sad? She couldn't be mean. Well, not hateful mean. Teasing mean was different. "No, you can come. If you want to."

"Uh, that's okay." His gaze dipped, and his lips curved down. "I know you don't really want me to go. It's been four days, and we've been joined at the hip since we crashed. You need a break."

Her shoulders sagged for a second, and then she smiled. "It's fine. This way, if something big tries to eat me, they can catch your slow rear first."

Zach lifted his gaze and smiled. "That's a mean thing to say, Harley Wilson."

"Hey, it's survival of the fittest out here."

He stood and brushed his hands on his swim trunks. "Where would you like to start?"

"I don't know. Let's just wander."

"Do you think we can get lost?"

That was a good point, but she had an excellent sense of direction. She was pretty sure she could keep it straight. "Well, we can leave markers as we go. Things that can't be moved by the wind."

"That works." He waved a hand toward the belly of the forest. "Ladies first."

She lifted her eyebrows. "Oh, no. I saw that movie. The girl gets hacked with a machete. You go first."

He rolled his eyes. "Would you come on."

"Fine, you big chicken."

"I swear, I'm—"

She stopped in front of him and raised her eyebrows. "You're what?"

His Adam's apple bobbed. "Uh."

"Yeah, that's what I thought." She quickly walked ahead of him, rolling her lips in to keep from laughing. The look on his face was worth millions. "Keep up, or I'll let you get lost."

Zach jogged to catch up to her and stuck his hands in his pockets. They walked a while in silence, making marks on trees deep enough they couldn't miss them when they started back to camp.

The island felt huge and so untamed. There were colorful birds, huge spiders, and little rodents that scurried from time to time. They'd even seen a snake or two. It'd given her the willies, but as long as they respected her personal space, she'd respect theirs.

Harley furrowed her brow. It almost sounded like rushing water was up ahead. "Do you hear that?"

"Sounds like water."

"Let's check it out." She took off toward the sound of the water, not waiting to see if he was keeping up with her. She'd only run a few feet when the trees parted and in front of her was a huge waterfall. Then she noticed she was standing on a rocky ledge and there was a whole ravine below her filled with all sorts of plants and birds. It was something out of a fantasy novel.

A moment later, Zach slid to a stop next to her. "Wow."

"Yeah."

"I never would've suspected this was here."

"Maybe we could find a way down." Harley shielded her eyes as she scanned the ravine. It was so pretty. The bright colors of the flowers stood out against the dark green foliage.

"Sure, that could be fun," he said and took a step forward. The rock gave way, and Harley didn't even think. She lunged forward and grabbed him around the waist, yanking him away from the ledge. They tumbled back onto the rocky ground, and she grunted as the rough surface scratched her leg and arm.

Her heart hammered in her chest as she lay on her back. She rolled onto her knees and leaned over Zach. "Are you okay?"

"Yeah, I'm fine," he said as he sat up. "Are you okay?"

"I'm okay. I—"

Zach pulled her into a bear hug and buried his face in her neck. Harley had to admit it felt good to be hugged like that. She circled her arms around his neck. If she hadn't lunged for him, he would have been gone. The drop down, with all the ragged rocks…There was no way he would have survived. Her desire to explore had evaporated too.

Second after second passed as he held her without saying a word, just his breath on her skin. Finally, he leaned back. "You've saved my life twice. At this rate, I'm going to have to hire you as my bodyguard."

What did she say to that? She didn't think about it. It was instinct, and she didn't like the idea of him being gone. No, she couldn't say that stuff. Besides, now that she'd saved him twice, he probably felt indebted to her or something. Instead of letting it get serious, she rolled her lips in and decided to be snarky. "At this rate, it'd be a short-lived job."

"You're not funny."

"Am too."

He rolled his eyes. "I'm catching dinner tonight."

"Okay, maybe you'll be better at it this time." She giggled.

They stood together, and she rubbed her arm where the ground had scratched it. Her thigh hurt too. She sneaked a peek at it as they walked back to camp. It was almost like an iron had been pressed to her skin. It burned like it too. She wasn't going to say anything, though. He'd probably feel guilty about that too, and she didn't want that.

Yeah, she'd pulled him back, but it was for selfish reasons. Mainly, she didn't want to be on the island by herself. The other reasons that whispered in her ear needed to put a sock in it.

"I'm catching one of these things if it's the last thing I do," Zach grumbled. He'd yet to catch anything, and every time he missed, Harley would giggle. Mean woman. He threw the spear again, and the fish zipped through his legs. He growled.

She threw her head back and laughed like it was the funniest thing she'd ever seen. "Give up?"

"No. I'm not giving up. I *am* catching dinner."

"If you say so," she said in a sing-song voice.

He pinched his lips together and pinned his gaze on the fish in the tide pool. She was never going to let him live it down if he didn't catch one. That'd be the first story she'd tell when they were found.

Zach took aim and threw the spear. It hit the target, and it was better than anything he'd ever done. He pulled the spear up and showed it to Harley. "See! I said I could do it."

She leaned over, hooked a finger in his shirt collar, and looked down it. "Huh."

"What are you doing?"

"Catch a few more, and you might actually have hair on your chest." She laughed. "Maybe I should take a count so we can see how many you grow per fish."

He knew she was being silly. Most likely, it was her way of easing his guilt at getting them stranded. He kinda liked it too. Being surrounded by stuffy people in suits got old, and it'd been forever since he'd felt so…light.

He clenched his jaw, pretending to be offended.

"I'm catching all of dinner tonight, even if it means we starve until breakfast."

"You should have a whole field of chest hair by then."

He rolled his eyes. "If I wasn't so hungry, I'd hold you down and tickle you until you cried."

She grinned. "You're a lot of talk for a man who can't catch fish."

With a renewed determination, he turned his sights on the fish swimming. He blocked out her little comments and concentrated. His next strike hit the target, and he pulled it up, putting the fish with the last one he'd caught. He repeated the same move seven more times and only missed once.

When the last one was caught, he smiled and crossed his arms over his chest. "Got anything to say now?"

"See? A little motivation is all you needed."

His face fell. "What?"

"I knew you could do it."

"You knew I could do it?"

"Of course I did. You just needed a little push."

She stood and patted his face. "Now, start a fire."

"You are one hard woman to please," he said, shaking his head as he lowered his gaze.

Harley picked up the fish and spun on her heels. "You coming?"

Zach stepped out of the pool and caught up with her. "You're still mean."

Her smile faltered. "Yeah, I guess I can be."

"I'm teasing you. Actually, you're the first person to push me like that." And now that he really thought about it, he liked that. Most people just let him skate. If he really dug deep, he was just as guilty.

She gave him a one-shoulder shrug. "You can do a lot more than you know. You just need to have the right person standing next to you sometimes."

He glanced at her. That wasn't something he'd ever considered. His parents' relationship was so contentious at the end that it was hard to see how they could have ever loved each other enough to get married. Had his mom stood next to his dad, pushing him to be better? Maybe he'd ask her when he got back home.

They reached camp, and Harley stopped at the edge. "I'll clean the fish, and you start the fire." She cupped his cheek and smiled. "I know you can do it."

His heart skipped a beat. "Okay." All he wanted at that moment was to start that fire, if for no other reason than to make her proud of him.

He did everything just the same as he had the time

before. It took him longer than he liked, but he had a fire going by the time she had the fish cleaned. He'd never been happier. Not just because he made her proud. He was proud of himself.

"See?"

He shook his head. "How did you know I could do it?"

"You just needed to know someone believed in you. That's all." She placed the fish on the fire and sat beside him.

The cobwebs had cleared, and a swarm of butterflies was free to dance in his stomach. It was a feeling he'd never had for a woman. Even the women he'd dated in college hadn't elicited that type of reaction in him. He didn't know what to think or say.

Harley braced her hands in the sand behind her, leaned back, and tipped her face to the sky. "I think I'm going to stay up tonight and do some stargazing. I bet the sky looks like it has glitter thrown in it. I've been so tired the last few days that I haven't even tried to enjoy them."

"Would you mind some company?"

"No, I wouldn't mind. Do you like stargazing?"

He chuckled. "I don't have a lot of time to do that back home."

"You can't work all the time. It'll burn you out. You

need to stop at the garden and slow down long enough to enjoy the fragrance."

Zach lay down on his side, facing her. "I tried trusting people to do things, and they didn't follow through. Once that happened a few times, I couldn't depend on anyone but myself."

She looked at him. "You can't stop trusting just because people fail. You keep trying until you find someone you can trust." She lowered her gaze, and a strange expression flashed across her face. A smile curved on her lips, but it felt like it was directed inward. "You can't give up." She lifted her gaze to his. "Because the person that comes along next might have been the one you needed the whole time. You just didn't know it."

"A lemons-to-lemonade philosophy?"

She sat up, pulled the fish off the fire, and slid a few his direction. "I guess you could say that. It just kind of hit me."

"How does it apply to you?"

Her gaze lifted to his and held it until he nearly flinched away.

"Something you won't tell me yet?"

She shook her head.

He wasn't sure what the key was to get past that

wall, but he wasn't giving up. Whatever he had to do to earn her trust, he'd do it. "Okay."

"You're not going to pressure me?"

"No. When you tell me, I want it to be because you want to."

Her eyes almost seemed to twinkle as she smiled. "Okay."

What flashed through his mind at that second nearly knocked him back. He liked Harley Wilson. He wanted her trust, her friendship, and more than anything, he wanted to get to know her better so he could fill in the details he'd been trying to ignore.

CHAPTER 12

Harley held his gaze a second longer before pulling away. She wanted to trust him, but she couldn't bring herself to tell him what happened with Samuel. The subject needed to move away from her. "You'd think eating fish for every meal for three days in a row would get old, but so far, I'm still liking it. I'm going to try to catch crabs again tomorrow."

"I have to agree. This hasn't been bad at all. Can't say I'll feel that way if we're here for a while."

"No, but if we do get tired of it, there are small animals on the island. Not that I'm keen on that, but it might keep us from going bonkers."

Harley stretched her legs out and sucked in a sharp breath. Her leg was sore and not just from the scratch. The muscle was tender, almost like it was bruised.

Zach knitted his eyebrows together. "What's wrong?"

"Nothing."

"You're not telling me the truth."

She didn't want to tell him. It's not like she would've done anything differently.

When she didn't respond, he took her chin in his fingers. "Tell me."

"I scratched my leg. It kinda hurts, but I'm fine."

"Which one?" She turned her left leg to him. "Did you get this when you pulled me from the ledge?" he asked.

"Yeah."

"Why didn't you say something?"

"I didn't want you to feel guilty or anything." She paused. "It's not like you made the ledge collapse."

He rubbed the back of his neck. "I do feel guilty, but it has nothing to do with you. Well, not you, you. Getting you stranded, yes, but that's not the whole of it. I feel useless here. I don't know if it's a guy thing or what, but I want to be the one taking care of you because I'm the one who got us into this situation."

Well, what did she say to that? He was taking care of her, in a way. If he wasn't there, she'd be really lonely. She covered his hand with hers. "It's okay. I kinda like this. I mean, it'd be comforting to know we had a definite date of departure, but being forced to slow down isn't so bad."

"And then you got hurt because of me."

Her lips slowly curved into a smile. "Selfish reasons, really."

"Oh, yeah?"

"Sure, if I'd let you fall, I'd have no one to tease. Talk about boring."

He shook his head. "You're mean." He palmed her leg just below the large scratch. "I don't know what to do to make this better."

Her skin tingled, and butterflies erupted in her stomach. His touch was sending her pulse skyward like a rocket. "It'll just have to heal on its own."

Zach pulled his hand away and looked upward. The sky was turning orange and red as the sun touched the ocean. "Ready to stargaze?"

"Yeah," she said and stood.

They walked a few feet and sat down. It was the same spot they used for cloud watching. It was shady enough to keep them out of the sun, but nothing blocked the sky.

"It's amazing what passes as entertainment when your choices are limited," Harley said. She did like the slow pace. Nothing was hurried. In Houston, everything was fast-paced.

Zach chuckled. "Yeah."

"You think someone will find us soon?" She squeezed her eyes shut. They'd just talked about him feeling guilty. Why did she ask that?"

"I don't know," he said, his voice soft as he lowered his gaze.

Harley hadn't meant to hurt him. She moved closer to him and touched his arm. "I'm so sorry. I was making conversation, and it just popped out."

"No, it's a good question. One I've been asking myself. By now, Matt should be wondering what happened. Hopefully, he's called Britney and she's got someone looking for us."

He sounded wounded. She tipped his chin up with her finger. The sadness in his eyes crushed her. "It's okay. We're going to be found. It's just a matter of time." She circled her arms around his neck. "It was a plane crash. You didn't do it on purpose. I'm not blaming you; I promise."

His arms wrapped around her and pulled her close. "I don't like failing. I don't like letting people down."

Without thinking, she kissed the side of his face, and for a second, she froze. When he didn't say anything, she said, "You haven't let anyone down."

He leaned back, and those amazing eyes of his locked with hers.

In an instant, her lungs were sucked empty. His lips were right there, and the temptation to kiss him was overwhelming. She shouldn't want to kiss him. He didn't know about Samuel. What if she kissed him and it was wonderful? What if he found out about Samuel and she'd never get to have any more of his wonderful kisses?

It was all out war between her head and her heart. He pressed his hand against the small of her back, and it slid up her spine until it rested on the back of her neck. Before she knew what was happening, he touched his lips to hers.

She wanted to pull away—should've pulled away—but the warmth of his body against her was enough to overshadow all the warnings sounding in her mind. He brushed his soft lips across hers, and she melted.

He pulled at her bottom lip with his teeth. A small moan escaped as he coaxed her lips to part. He deepened the kiss, and it was more heavenly than any kiss she'd experienced. His touch was so gentle, like every piece of her was something worth taking time to treasure.

No, her head screamed. He was kissing her because she'd saved his life. It was an illusion of feelings. Harley broke the kiss.

Zach looked at her, his eyes stormy.

"I'm sorry. I think it's too easy to get confused here." She tried to move away, but he captured her in his arms.

"I'm not confused."

"I am, and I don't think this is a good idea."

He nodded. "Okay," he said and cupped her cheek, rubbing his thumb across her lips. "I want to hold you. Would that be okay?"

Could she handle being held by him? Would she want more than that if she did let him hold her? "Okay."

Zach pulled her onto his lap and held her against him. His heart beat furiously under her hand and matched the unsteady rhythm of her own. He tipped her chin up and softly pressed his lips to her forehead.

She didn't say another word. If she did, she wasn't sure she wouldn't kiss him. His warmth was addictive, and she couldn't let herself get caught up in whatever was happening. Tomorrow, she'd have a clear head. Tomorrow, she'd keep her distance.

ALL NIGHT LONG, the second his eyes would close, Zach was kissing Harley again. It was like he'd put it on repeat. Not once had his mind allowed him to drift off.

He had no idea what happened. In less than a heartbeat, he went from telling himself, *Don't do it,* to pressing his lips to hers. Her lips were softer than he could have imagined. Then she'd responded to the kiss, and it was amazing.

Part of him wanted to attribute it to his firm stance on no relationships the last few years, but there was no way that was it, and he knew it. Every second the kiss continued, he felt more and more that it wasn't just the kiss, but the person he was sharing it with. There was something different about this woman, and despite his unwillingness to admit it, he couldn't deny it now. There was some unknown...something drawing him to her.

The kiss started so fast and ended just as quickly. The disappointment that fell over him when she pulled back crushed him. Didn't she feel the connection? Maybe she didn't. Or maybe she did, and she was scared. Were his own feelings real? She'd saved his life. Twice. If she hadn't, would that change how he felt about her?

He'd kissed her without thinking about it. It was unplanned, and now he was more confused than he'd ever been in his life. When he'd left Houston, relationship was a four-letter word. His mom tried to tell him he shouldn't let his father taint his opinion of being with someone, but his mom didn't see how stricken she'd look when his father hurt her.

Harley took a soft breath and shifted in his arms. He looked down at her sleeping form. She'd drifted off as they watched the stars. Once he was sure she was in a deep sleep, he'd moved them into the shelter. Now, he was watching her as the sun inched its way over the horizon.

She shifted again, this time sighing as she hooked her arm over his chest. He touched his lips to her forehead. It was a natural reaction. There wasn't even a moment's hesitation.

Her eyes opened, and for a heartbeat, she stared at him.

"Good morning," he said.

A smile slowly formed on her lips, and she rubbed her thumb under his eyes. "You didn't sleep well."

"I'm fine. Did you sleep okay?"

She nodded. "Um, about last night—"

"Don't worry about it. We'll chalk it up to island sickness."

For a split second, her smile faltered. "That's probably a good idea."

"How's your leg doing?" he asked.

She lowered her gaze and touched her fingertips to the scratch. "It hurts, but not as bad as yesterday."

What he wouldn't give to have some way of making it better. He hated that she'd been hurt because of him.

"Hey," she said and tipped his chin up. Her eyes seemed to see right through him. "It's okay."

"It doesn't feel okay."

Her lips curved up. "But it is, and I'd do it again."

Zach nodded. "All right. Are you hungry?"

She shot him a grin and sat up. "Are you doing the catching?"

"Are you going to tease me while I do it?" Zach asked as he pushed himself into a sitting position.

"Probably."

Zach threw his back and laughed. "You're so mean."

She giggled in response. "Yeah, but you catch them better when I am."

"Fine," he said and untangled himself from her like he was upset.

"Oh, don't you start your pouting. I know it's a trick. You just want to tickle me."

He crossed his arms over his chest and turned his back to her. "I'm not pouting." He quickly glanced over his shoulder.

Harley pressed herself into his back as she hugged

him around the neck. "You stink at pouting, but you sure are cute."

He twisted to look at her and regretted it. Those plump rosy lips were right there. The same temptation from the night before hit him, and his mouth went dry. No. She was right. The island was making things confusing. He quickly pulled himself together and grinned. "You think so, huh?"

"Like you don't know it."

"Maybe I just like to hear it. You ever think of that?"

She rolled her eyes and shook her head. "Fine. You're absolutely adorable."

"Now, was that so hard?"

"Awful."

"I stand by my statement. You're mean, and if I wasn't starving, I'd tickle you."

She took a deep breath and let it out slowly. "Come on, tickle monster, let's get breakfast."

The way she was looking at him, the wide grin on her lips, made it impossible to not think about kissing her. She was full of light and life. Who could have ever thought she was someone to throw away? How could they spend any time with her and not want more of her?

Harley crawled out of the shelter and stood. "Well, are you coming?"

"Yeah, I'm coming." He came out of the shelter and stopped next to her. If he could, he'd put his arms around her and kiss her. All his talk of island madness was stupid. He'd liked holding her and kissing her. It had nothing to do with her saving him and everything to do with how he felt when she was near.

Then again, how was he sure that was what he was really feeling? He hadn't felt that way about a woman before. Not even close. So, what was causing all the doubts? Maybe he needed to figure that out first before he let himself kiss her again.

CHAPTER 13

Harley fell back onto the sand, laughing harder than she had in years. Zach was trying so hard, and it was so cute. He'd done pretty well the day before, even if it had taken a little while. She didn't know why he was struggling so much now.

"Stop laughing," he said. His lips pinched together, and he looked so grumpy.

"Stop being so funny!" She rolled to her side, still laughing, and held her stomach. He was hysterical. Every time he'd miss, he'd grumble.

She scanned the bare sand and sat up. "You know what we haven't done?"

"What?"

"If someone flies over and happens to miss the wreckage, they won't know we're here. I don't know how I forgot that. It should have been one of the first things we did." She stood and turned in place. "We need rocks and a pyre. If we see someone coming, we light it, and they'll see it."

"Okay."

"We'll eat first then do that."

His shoulders sagged. "Great."

"You thought you'd get out of fishing, huh?"

He pinched his lips shut, and his eyebrows knitted together. She'd learned over the last few days that it was his determination face. It was funny and cute. Well, all of him was cute.

"No," he said. "I'm just figuring out my strategy."

Harley rocked back and forth on her heels. "I know. I'm messing with you. You've gotten pretty good."

"I'm slow as all get out."

"Yeah, but slow is better than nothing."

"I'm not used to being slow." He narrowed his eyes and then threw the spear. When he picked it up, a fish was on the end. He pulled it off and set it on the sand.

She smiled and clapped. "Slow and steady wins the race."

"Are you calling me a tortoise?"

"Yes."

He rolled his eyes and went back to fishing.

"You know, you could let me fish."

"That's okay. I don't mind." He speared another fish and set it down with the other one. "It makes me feel like I'm contributing."

Something in his voice made her stop and watch him. There was a sadness clinging to him. She walked to the tide pool and stepped into it.

He whirled around and faced her.

"What makes you think you aren't contributing? You've been doing all the fishing and making all the fires since you learned how. I think that's contributing."

"I don't know."

"We're a team on this island. Nothing is fifty-fifty all the time. It can't be. Sometimes, it's sixty-forty. Sometimes it's thirty-seventy. As long as neither of us gives up, what difference does it make if we're not even all the time?"

Zach's gaze dipped to the water. "I feel like I need to make up for the first day."

"Oh, Zach, you're thinking like someone who's keeping score. I'm not. I don't want to. It's too much work. You don't do things out of obligation. You do things because it's in your heart to do them. That's what makes them mean something. Why did you take that equipment to Matt?"

"I knew I could help, and I wanted to. It made me happy to know I'd done something worthwhile with my time and money."

"There ya go. You do it because it makes you happy. Are you keeping count of all the things Matt does for you?"

He kneaded his eyebrows together. "Well, no. He doesn't have money or anything. He's a volunteer doctor who barely makes a wage."

"Okay, when he talks to you, is he always asking for something?"

"No, and he didn't really ask the first time. I volunteered when he told me what he was doing."

Harley grinned inside and out. This man was nothing like Samuel Baldwin. Samuel would make sure Matt repaid him somehow. She pressed the palm of her hand over his heart. "You're a good man, Zachary Wolf. Stop worrying about whether you're scoring high enough or not."

As he held her gaze, he covered her hand with his. "You're the first person to ever say something like that to me."

She pulled her hand free and stepped out of the tidal pool. "You finish catching breakfast, and then we'll get our S.O.S. made."

Zach nodded and went back to work. Once he'd

caught enough, they went back to camp and ate. When they were finished, they walked along the edge of the beach.

"So, tell me about your sisters and brothers," Harley said as they looked for rocks large enough to be seen from the sky.

Zach chuckled. "Uh, well, there's Britney. She's the baby. And she can be a little ditzy, but most of the time it's cute. She's funny, outgoing, sweet, down to earth, and she has a way of putting anyone at ease. I don't think she knows what the word enemy means."

"I think I'd like her."

"Oh, you'd get along great."

"And your other sister?"

"Zoe is the oldest and the opposite of Britney. She is quick-witted, organized, and she doesn't put up with much. My father groomed her to take over the company, but she didn't want to. I wanted it, and she went behind his back and taught me everything."

Harley's mouth dropped open. "What about your brothers? He didn't want them to take it over?"

"Julian is six years older than me and not what you'd call business-minded. He's a painter, musician, and a complete free spirit. The minute he was able to move away, he did."

"And your other brother?"

"Noah. I don't know. He's next in age to me. I think he wanted it until my father started changing. Once that happened, he pulled away. He's an Army Ranger. One of the youngest ever."

"So your father wasn't always horrible to your mom or you?"

"No," he said it so softly that it almost sounded wistful.

"What happened to Noah?"

"I think it broke him. He and my father were the closest, despite him grooming Zoe to take over. Then one day, something happened. They'd gone on a trip together, and when they got back, they weren't speaking to each other. That's when things got bad."

"Noah wouldn't tell you what happened?"

Zach shook his head. "No, I don't think he's ever told anyone."

"Not even your mom?"

"If he did, she didn't tell any of us."

"Are any of your siblings married?"

"Zoe married two years ago. If everything goes as planned, I'll be an uncle this fall."

Harley smiled. "Oh, that's exciting. How do you feel about being an uncle?"

"I don't know. Part of me thinks it'll be great, and the other worries I won't be good enough."

"Oh, that's silly. You're plenty good enough."

He shot her a smile that made her stomach flutter. "You think so?"

"I know so."

"How do you know?"

She shrugged. "I just do. A so-so guy wouldn't have been taking equipment to a foreign country to help his friend with cleft palate surgeries."

"That's all?"

"Well, you'll have to rescue a kitten or something to get better."

He threw his head back and laughed. "I'll keep that in mind."

That laugh. Man, she liked that laugh. It was so rich and warm and felt like it came from deep within. That's why she teased him. She couldn't get enough of it. Oh man, they needed to get off the island before she got her heart broken again.

"How about your other siblings?"

"Oh, well, Julian was close once. He's dating someone now, and I've met her a couple times. She seems to get him. I think this one might work out."

"Noah?"

"He…plays the field, or he likes people to think he does."

"Why?"

Zach took a deep breath. "My parents' divorce hit all of us in different ways. With Zoe, it made her more determined to make a relationship work. Julian wasn't there during the worst of it, so it didn't affect him as badly. Noah likes to pretend it didn't affect him, but I know it did. Anytime there's a hint someone might get close, he ends it. I don't know about Britney. She dates from time to time. I tell her the right one is out there. If that's what she wants."

"And you?"

He shrugged. "I don't…I don't have relationships. I don't want one."

She lifted her eyebrows. "You've never been in a relationship, then?"

"I was." He braced his hand against a tree and looked up. "I ended it." A heartbeat later, he added, "I don't want what happened to my parents' to happen to me. I don't want to love someone for thirty years and then one day watch them just turn into a different person. I'd rather be single."

Harley knew it was just the island and rescuing him that had him acting all sweet. He'd kissed her because he felt obligated. He didn't really want her; it was this place. At least she knew. She'd heard it from his own lips now, and she could keep a clear head. "I can understand that. It's hard when you see what you believe to be a solid relationship disintegrate."

"Yeah, it is." He cleared his throat. "Okay, enough about me," he said as he began walking again. "You said your mom is really organized. Are you the same way?"

Harley nearly choked. "No. Well, I am, just not as obsessive as she is. For her, everything has a place and the place has a label."

"What does she do for a living?"

"She's a professional organizer."

"Guess I should have known that."

She shrugged. "I'm kidding. She's a bank manager in Lubbock." Her mom had started at the bottom as a teller. She worked anytime they needed someone, even if it meant there were times she'd have to postpone things they had planned. It didn't bother Harley. She knew how badly her mom wanted to feel accomplished. Once she moved to an accounts position, she'd started taking online college classes. It took her six years, but she graduated with a bachelor's in finance.

"I can see organizational skills coming in handy for that type of work."

"She's worked super hard to be where she is. I'm proud of her." The day she was promoted, they celebrated with a huge party. Her mom looked so proud. Harley would never forget the look on her face.

"Did you try college?"

"Uh, I did, but it wasn't for me. I love what I do. It's fun, and it makes people happy."

Zach nodded. "I can understand that."

"Really?"

"Sure, if I didn't like what I do, it'd be hard to show up to work every day."

That was different. The only reason Samuel had been okay with it was because it didn't interfere with the plans he'd make.

Zach shot Harley a quick glance. His heart had been racing since their talk that morning. Everyone kept score. Well, everyone but her, and there was no doubt she wasn't keeping a tally. Not once had it even felt like she was, either. He didn't know why it was so important to him to balance things out.

Because if he was honest, he wasn't trying to make things even. He wanted to take care of her. The thought sent a jolt through him. Until he remembered telling her he didn't want a relationship. It'd just slipped off his tongue like it was nothing. He was so used to saying it that it was like a scripted line.

The moment it left his lips, he'd noticed a difference in her tone and the way she held herself, like she'd put up an invisible wall. Could he blame her? He'd essentially done the same thing by telling her he wasn't interested. How cheesy would it be to tell her she'd changed his thoughts on dating and relationships? Did he know what he wanted? Yeah, the kiss had been great. No, it'd been fireworks, but did that really change anything?

"Zach?"

He startled. "What?"

"I've been calling your name. What's got you in deep thought?"

Like he'd blab that. "Nothing, just looking for rocks."

"Uh, huh."

"You say that like you don't believe me."

She lifted an eyebrow. "Like you believed me yesterday?"

"Oh, yeah, what *were* you going to say?"

Harley rolled her lips in and shook her head.

"Then I'm not telling either," he said.

She narrowed her eyes, and in a split second, she dropped the stones she'd picked up and ran toward him. Her fingers darted up his sides and around his middle. "I told you I'd get you back."

Zach reached for her, and it seemed like she'd dance away, just out of reach, before pouncing on him again. "Oh, when I get my hands on you…"

"If," she said in that sing-song tone of hers, taunting him.

He needed a different tactic. The next time she tickled him, he pretended to trip and fall.

"Zach?"

He groaned and held his leg.

"Are you tricking me?" she asked.

Sucking in a sharp breath, he grunted as he sat up, still holding his leg.

Harley muttered and walked to him. "I know you're probably faking."

The second she was in reach, he grabbed her and pulled her down. "You've got your ways, and I've got mine."

"You're a faker, Zachary Wolf!" she squealed as he tickled her.

"Yes, I am, but I caught you." He pinned her arms above her head and tickled her a little more before giving her a breather.

She panted and tried to squirm out of his grip. "You just wait. I'll get you."

"So you say."

When she stopped fighting him, she shook her head. "You don't play fair."

His mouth dropped open. "*I* don't play fair? You don't play fair."

"I play fair. I'm just teasing. You're the one who wants to tickle me until I cry."

Zach let go of her hands. "Okay, so maybe we're even."

She sat up and drew her knees to her chest, pulling the end of the t-shirt over her legs as she did. "We should probably look for rocks again."

"Yeah, probably," he said and stood, holding his hand out to her.

Harley took his hand, and he pulled her up. She went to the pile of rocks she'd dropped and gathered them up again. "So, you said you grew up in Houston, right?"

"Yep, I've lived there my whole life. I couldn't imagine living somewhere else," he said and stooped to pick up a rock he knew Harley couldn't carry.

"I felt that way about Lubbock until I moved here."

"But you want to move back? Didn't you mention that?" For some unknown reason, that bothered him.

She nodded. "Yeah, I realized a few months ago that I don't belong in Houston. Plus, I miss my family."

"Of course you belong in Houston. Everyone does. Have you made any friends yet?"

"No, not really."

"I'm sorry to hear that. And, to be honest, I find it hard to believe."

A little shrug of her shoulder. "I thought I had, but it turns out they weren't who I thought they were."

"I get that. I say I have friends, but they're more like acquaintances. Well, except for my friend in Jamaica. Matt Rivers is a good friend. He thinks about more than himself."

Harley smiled. "I guess having money would make it hard to know who your friends are."

"That, and the people I grew up with are all…well, they have different ideas than I do."

She tilted her head. "How so?"

How did he explain it in a way that didn't sound like the typical woe-is-me rich guy? "My grandfather had nothing when he started this company. Within a year, his life had changed. The people I grew up with have never wanted for anything in their lives. I haven't either, but my grandfather made sure I knew where I came from. I want to give back. I want to be remembered for more than being wealthy. I want to be remembered for doing something that matters."

"I think we all want that."

He lifted his gaze to hers, and a brilliant smile played on her lips.

"How about you?" he asked.

She shrugged. "I had some friends in Lubbock, but since I moved to Houston, we've lost touch."

"When did you move to Houston?"

"About a year and a half ago. I wanted a change of scenery. The first thing I did when I got here was go to all the art exhibits."

Zach grinned. "I can see that."

"There was this one for Theo Norse, and I was amazed by his stuff. I helped Trixie plan the party for his opening night."

"What was the name?"

"Theo Norse."

His mouth dropped open. "No way. I went to that exhibit. I think I would have remembered seeing you."

"I was behind the scenes most of the time."

"True." He thought for a second. "I think I remember Sam saying something about meeting someone at that exhibit." He returned his attention to Harley, and an unreadable expression flashed across her features.

CHAPTER 14

The mention of Samuel's name made her stomach twist. "Are you two close?" She wasn't sure why she asked that. Did she want to know? Not really, but it was a logical follow-up question.

He shook his head. "Not what I'd call close, but if I needed furniture moved, I'd ask for his help. Of course, knowing him, he'd hire it out. The guy hates hard labor."

"Did he end up dating that someone?" she asked as nonchalantly as she could. Since Samuel never returned her phone calls, she didn't know how it had affected him. All she had was that letter, and the only tone it had was the one she gave it.

"You know, I think so. I also remember getting a

wedding invitation several months ago, but the wedding was called off."

The lump in her throat grew, and she swallowed hard. "That's sad."

"Are you okay?"

Harley nodded. "Oh yeah. Just sad for your friend. Did he say why it was called off? Did they just decide against it?"

"It was a couple months after that before I spoke to him, probably two months ago. It must have been a mutual decision. I asked him about it, and he acted like it was nothing. Said that he'd moved on, and then he started talking about his dad's company."

Mutual? Like nothing had happened. Harley felt the color drain from her face. "Uh, well, that's good. At least it wasn't a nasty breakup." For Samuel.

"Are you sure you're okay?"

"I'm fine," she said and forced her best smile. Her heart was aching so bad it felt like it was the epicenter of an earthquake. "I'm going to unload these on the beach so I can get more."

Zach returned her smile. "Okay. I probably need to dump the ones I have too."

"Sure." A tear streaked down Harley's cheek as she turned away from him and walked to the beach. The last thing she wanted to do was break down in front of

Zach again. Stupid tears. Hadn't she cried enough for Samuel Baldwin? Samuel hadn't hurt even a little after leaving her? How could he tell her he loved her and then not have so much as a little remorse?

"Harley?" Zach called.

There was no way she could face him right now. Not as weepy as she was. Her heart felt like it'd been kicked. She dropped her rocks and took off down the beach and then veered into the forest.

"Harley!" His voice sounded so urgent and full of concern.

She couldn't answer him, so she continued to run. It was a blur of trees and foliage as she picked up speed, racing away from Zach. Even if she had to explain it later, it'd be better than at the present.

It didn't matter how fast she ran, she couldn't get away from the hurt. She slowed to a stop and braced her hands on her thighs as she gulped air. More tears streamed down her face as she realized Samuel had left her and he didn't care a bit how it had hurt her. How could he look her in the eyes and tell her he loved her and then not feel anything?

Harley lowered herself to the ground as her memories played. When she looked back on it with a critical eye, it wasn't as great as she'd wanted to believe.

He never introduced her when they went to functions. He'd say it was because he knew she was nervous. When he did introduce her, it was at events where his parents were in attendance. Dates were at her apartment. He'd said it was because he didn't want to share her. Was that even true?

Now that she thought about it, he'd proposed to her in front of his parents at a huge event they'd hosted. When he'd asked her, he didn't get on one knee. No, he'd spoken to the crowd like he was some game show host. At the time, it'd bothered her, but he loved her and that's what mattered. She'd shrugged it off as being the way rich people did things.

Even after he'd proposed and put the ring on her finger, it'd been less about her and more about the people watching. Once the evening was over, it was like nothing happened. Over the next six months, she was the one who got the guest list together. She was the one who got the venue. He hadn't gone with her. At the time, he said he was too busy with work. But he hadn't helped with anything. It'd all been her—all of it.

The realization left her breathless. She'd been so stupid. He'd never loved her. She'd been so caught up in wanting to be loved that she'd let things slide. But why would he have asked her to marry him if he didn't love her? It made no sense. Who did that?

A flame of anger settled in the pit of her stomach.

She'd cried for that jerk. For two whole months. Her good jeans didn't fit because she'd stuffed her face with so much ice cream. Oh, she was so done crying. Not only had the island helped her officially get over Samuel, it'd probably got her back in her jeans too.

Harley blew out a puff of air and let her head drop back. Why had it taken her so long to figure it out? She sighed. Because it hurt to know he'd never loved her, and she hadn't been willing to confront it. Well, she'd done it now, and surprisingly, she was okay. No, she was better than okay. And if she ever saw Samuel Baldwin again, he'd get a good old-fashioned dose of Harley Wilson. That uppity cuss wouldn't know what hit him, either.

How could Zach be friends with Samuel? Zach did say he wasn't the best of friends with the people he grew up with. Maybe that applied to Samuel. Zach didn't outright say it, though, so she couldn't assume he included Samuel in that statement.

Although, the way Zach described his family, they weren't anything like the Baldwins. That's if he was telling the truth. Sometimes the truth was what someone wanted it to be. She couldn't blame him if that was the case. Hadn't she done that with Samuel?

Maybe she should tell Zach what happened. Wouldn't he figure it out anyway? All he'd have to do was ask Samuel when they got home. It wasn't like it was some big secret. Okay, so it was, but only because she'd let it be. The thought made her even angrier. She'd let that jerk stick her in a corner like some broken vase not worthy to be out in the open.

It wasn't like she had a shot with Zach. He'd been absolutely clear with his feelings about relationships. And even if she had a shot with him, if he let Samuel's opinion of her influence him, then good riddance.

Those jerks were done telling her what she was worth. They could all jump in a lake. What made them so great anyway? Money? She scoffed. Whatever. It was only their high-and-mighty opinion of themselves, and that didn't mean anything to her. Not anymore.

A smile curved on her lips, and she chuckled. She'd come to her senses, and all it'd taken was a plane crash. She needed to get back to camp. They needed to get their beach distress signal made and get off this island.

She lowered her gaze to the forest floor and smiled. A few rocks littered the ground a few feet to her right. They were larger than the ones they'd been finding. "At least I didn't run for nothing," she said as she stood.

Once she'd picked up all she could carry, she

headed back to camp. The foliage was a lot thicker there than the rest of the island. Little branches that had been snapped off from the last storm littered the ground. She stepped over one, and something pricked her foot. When she lifted it, she took a glance and decided it was most likely just a thorn. She'd check it out better when she got to camp.

ONE FULL "S" and half an "O," and Zach had run out of rocks. Sure, he could find more, but it wasn't as fun looking for them when Harley wasn't around. He didn't even know where she'd gone.

The last time he'd seen her, she was walking to the beach. He'd called her name, and then she was just gone. After a while, when she still hadn't returned, he'd gone looking for her and couldn't find her anywhere.

Zach pushed through the brush and walked back into camp. He'd hoped she'd come back while he was gone, but no such luck. He reached the edge and sat down hard on the sand as he raked his hand through his hair.

He knew something was wrong, but he didn't

expect her to just leave without saying a word. Or to be gone so long.

Everything was fine until…until he started talking about Sam. Her voice had sounded off after that. After saying Sam had been fine about his marriage being called off.

Harley went to that Norse exhibit. Sam dated someone he'd met there. Zach squeezed his eyes shut. Oh, he was thick. That's why she'd been so icy after they'd taken off from the airport. That's why she'd been so upset when he'd called her amazing. She said she'd been around people like him. No, people with money.

How did he not see it sooner? There was a chance he was putting the puzzle together wrong, but the way she reacted to things made him pretty confident he'd figured it out. Sam had called off their wedding. He'd made it sound like it was mutual, but gauging by the way Harley behaved, it wasn't.

Why would Sam ask her to marry him and then back out? Maybe there was a side to her Zach hadn't seen yet. They'd only been on the island five days. Granted, they'd had nothing but each other, and they'd talked a lot. But that didn't mean he knew her well enough to bet farms or anything.

He stood and walked until he was ankle-deep in

the water, letting his feet get buried in the sand as it covered them. No, he did know her, and he couldn't understand Sam treating her like that. Man, he hoped she'd trust him enough to tell him what happened.

"Zach."

He turned, and he'd never been more relieved to see someone. She stood a few feet from him with her arms full of rocks. "Harley, where have you been? I looked everywhere for you."

All she did was stare at him. Then the rocks tumbled out of her arms as she dropped them to her side.

He took a step toward her. "Can you give me some sort of answer?" He tilted his head as he studied her. Now that he was really looking at her, she looked flushed. "Harley, what's wrong?"

She blinked a few times. Her mouth opened. "I—"

Then her knees buckled, and Zach couldn't move fast enough. He caught her before she hit the sand, and she was like a rag doll in his arms. "Harley?" He held her face in his hand. Her skin was so hot. "Harley?"

Zach picked her up, carried her through camp, and didn't stop until he was at the spring. He waded out into it and lowered her into the water.

"No," she said and latched her arms around his neck. "Too cold," she cried.

Oh, he hated to do it. Not when she sounded like that. "We need to bring your body temperature down." He waded out further and further until she was submerged to her chest. "Where were you?"

Instead of an answer, her arms fell from his neck, and he knew she'd passed out. He waded back out and sat down with her on his lap in water deep enough to cover her. He tipped her head back and trickled water over it. Then he dripped some into her mouth.

What had happened? She was the one to tell him to stay out of the sun. He looked over the length of her body and stopped at her left foot. It was swollen, and dark lines curled around it. She'd been stung by something, and he had no idea what it could be.

At the moment, all he knew to do was to get her temperature down. Beyond that, he had no idea. He brushed the back of his hand across her cheek. She had to be okay, right?

CHAPTER 15

The dreams were warm and pleasant. They swirled around her like a soft caress. One second she was at her mom's home in Lubbock, labeling the Cocoa Puffs and organizing canned goods. In another dream, she was camping with her grandma. Harley could feel her presence. The next dream, she was watching a movie with Zach and eating popcorn.

Her last dream was the best. She was leaned back against him while he was kissing her neck and combing his fingers through her hair. She turned and threw her arms around his neck. It was heaven. His warmth. His care. Him. Oh, she wanted him.

When the last dream dissolved, everything ached. She hurt down into the marrow of her bones. Her insides felt like they were being cooked. Then her stomach clenched like someone was reaching in and squeezing it. With a groan, she opened her eyes. It felt like her muscles were on fire as she tried to move her arm and she whimpered.

"Oh, thank goodness you woke up." Zach leaned over her, and his face slowly came in to focus. "I've spent two days trying to keep your fever down."

"It hurts to move," she whispered.

"You were stung by something."

"I'm hot, and I don't feel good." She tried to move again and stopped short.

Zach cupped her cheek. "I know. Are you thirsty? I went to the wreckage and found some glasses and even a pitcher. We didn't need to before…"

"I'm…I'm thirsty."

He lifted her and tipped the glass to her lips. The water wasn't hot, but it wasn't icy either. Still, it quenched her dry mouth.

"Your temperature is really high again."

When he laid her back down, it felt like a weight was set on top of her chest. She gasped for air and choked. "I…can't…breathe," she said between each gulp of air.

Zach lifted her again, set her against his chest, and began rubbing her back. "Keep fighting."

Her chest hurt. All of her hurt. It suddenly felt like someone was jabbing her with needles.

"Come on, Harley, just keep fighting, okay?"

She wanted to keep fighting, but she hurt so bad. The fire in her muscles felt like an all-consuming wildfire. Her eyes slid shut as she sucked in breath after breath. It felt like her ribs were being broken.

"I'm sorry to do this to you."

Harley felt him lift her. Felt the momentum of being carried.

"I'm so sorry. You're not going to like this."

The moment the water hit her body, she tried to scream, but it caught in her throat. It was like she was in a freezer. Her muscles contracted, her body trembled, and all she wanted to do was float away from the pain. Before she went, though, she had a few things to say. The frayed thread holding her tightened as her thoughts formed.

Harley needed her mom to know she loved her. All of her. That she didn't mind her kitchen being rearranged. That she was proud of all her mom's hard work and accomplishments. All the sacrifices she made.

"Zach."

"Yeah?"

"Would you tell…would you tell my mom that I love her?"

He cupped her head and leaned back. "No. You'll tell her. We're getting off this island, both of us, together. And when we do, I'm throwing a huge party. You have to be there for it to be a party worth having."

"P-please."

"No," he said. His voice sounded so strained.

She forced her eyes open as far as she could. Those eyes, like blue pen lights, stared straight at her. She slid her hand up his chest and touched his lips. "I…I shouldn't have stopped you from kissing me."

"Then stick around. It'll be mean if I don't get to kiss you again."

The idea of being kissed by him again brought a tiny smile to her lips. If she could, she'd kiss him right that second. Why did she have to run away earlier? "I am mean," she said as her eyes closed. She'd had no energy to start with, and it felt like the little light inside her was being blown out.

Zach's arms were around her and his mouth against her ear, and the last thing she heard was, "Please stay." His voice cracked. "Just stay."

If she could stay, she would. For him.

Zach didn't consider himself to be an emotional guy, but Harley had gutted him. Asking him to tell her mom she loved her? He'd felt stabbed through the heart. There was no way he could do that. Not only was it his fault they were stranded, but now he might be responsible for her…he couldn't bring himself to say the word. Just the thought made it difficult to breathe.

Then her lips had curved into a tiny smile. Wishing she'd let him continue kissing her. Telling him she was mean. Her eyes slid shut, and it was almost like he could feel her slipping away. He was sure she hadn't heard him begging her to stay.

He'd decided then and there that he didn't care what Sam had to say. Whatever his reason for calling off the wedding, it had worked in Zach's favor. In fact, when he saw Sam the next time, he'd thank him for being an idiot. Maybe he'd even invite him to the party after they were found so he could do just that.

His rules about relationships had taken a backseat. He had feelings for her, and they had nothing to do with her saving his life. His feelings for her had only to do with her quirky, sweet self.

By the time her blistering skin was cooled enough to pull her out of the water, his legs felt like ice cubes. It was worth it, though. As her temperature came down, her breathing became less labored. He'd never been so happy in his life to listen to someone breathe.

That's what he did when he returned to camp with her. For hours, he sat against a tree with her in his arms, listening to her breathe like it was "Moonlight Sonata" and every lungful of air she took was a precious note.

She stirred and took a deep breath. "Hi," she whispered.

A brick-sized lump formed in his throat. "Hey," he choked out.

"Are you okay?"

He almost laughed. She'd nearly died, and her first question was to ask if he was okay? "Yeah, how are you feeling?"

She groaned. "Like I got beat up and backed over with a truck. I'm achy all over."

"I know you are." He'd watched as her muscles twitched while she was passed out. Whatever stung her had hit her system hard. That she'd survived was a testament to her strength.

"Do you remember what happened?"

Harley braced her hand against his chest, trying to sit up, but fell back against him. "I thought I stepped on a twig, but I knew it was a sting when my leg went numb."

"How did you make it back to camp?"

"I don't know," she said through a yawn. "I just remember I had to get back because I needed to tell you something."

He wrapped his arms around her and kissed the top of her head. "Tell me later."

His shirt moved up and down as she nodded. "Okay."

"You want some water?" He'd kept the pitcher and a glass next to him in the hopes that she'd wake up and want some.

She nodded again.

He poured her a glass of water and put it to her lips. She greedily drank it and the next two he offered. "You were a little thirsty."

"I didn't realize how dry my mouth was." This time when she braced her hands against his chest, she managed to sit up. "Thank you for taking care of me."

Like he had a choice? Not because he felt like he owed her, but because he didn't want to lose her. He smiled and smoothed her hair back. "For once, I felt useful on this island."

Her arms circled his neck, and she brushed her lips across his cheek as she rested her head against his shoulder. "Oh, you underestimate your worth, Zach. You mean the world to me."

His skin broke out in goosebumps as her lips moved against his neck. The last sentence made his heart race. He wrapped his arms around her and hugged her close. She was still sick. There was no way she knew what she was saying or meant it.

Plus, one of the last conversations they had was him telling her he didn't want a relationship. Since he'd been with her, all of his rules had been challenged. He didn't know what he wanted anymore. The only thing he was absolutely sure of was that he was falling for her.

The more logical part of his brain yelled at him that things would be different if he wasn't on the island. That once they were found and back in Houston, he'd come to his senses and things would go back to normal.

Except his heart couldn't imagine that being the case. The longer he was with Harley, the more space she took up. He liked how she filled that space, too. Her smile, her laughter, her teasing. The parts of his heart he'd quarantined from the world were begging for her.

"I think I could sit like this forever," she whispered. "Just being held." She took a deep breath, and as she did, her body sagged.

Zach touched his lips to her forehead and said,

"Yeah, me too." He looked up and said a silent prayer that someone would find them soon. If not, he was going to lose all his resolve. He needed to get back to civilization. He needed solid ground and not some fantasy created by an unrealistic situation.

Once he got back to Houston, he could take a step back and analyze things. Then he'd know what he wanted.

CHAPTER 16

The smell of fish cooking woke Harley. Her stomach growled like she hadn't eaten for a year. She pushed herself into a sitting position and groaned. Every muscle she had protested. It felt like she'd been pounded with a meat tenderizer. She cast her gaze to her leg. The swelling was mostly gone, and the dark lines were fading.

Zach had his back to her, sitting in front of the campfire. He turned and smiled. "Hey," he said, weariness lacing the word.

She hauled herself from the shelter and sat beside him. "Hi. Look at you. Catching fish and making fires." Her breath caught as he looked at her. His eyes were bloodshot with dark circles around them. "You didn't sleep at all?"

He shook his head. "I couldn't. Not until I was sure you were okay. I was afraid if I did, you'd stop breathing or something."

Her mouth dropped open. He'd lost sleep because he was worried about her? "How long have you been up?"

"Uh, it's been three days. This is the first time you've been coherent since the last time you passed out."

Three days? "And you caught fish?"

He shrugged. "I thought maybe you'd be hungry when you woke up. I wanted you to be able to eat. I figured it'd take you another day to feel a hundred percent."

"You look like you're about to fall over."

"Nah, I'm all right."

She nodded. He was far from all right. He looked haggard. "How did you know when to put the fish on?"

"I didn't. My plan was to wake you up when it was done, but I think the smell woke you up." He pulled the largest fish off and handed it to her. "Eat that one first. He's big, but he took forever to catch, and I've learned not to dine on the corpses of my enemies."

Harley laughed, and it came from all the way down in her stomach. "You know, you could have a little bite." She pulled a piece off and offered it to him. "I mean, he's big after all, and it'll add to that chest hair you're trying to grow."

Zach chuckled, put his arm around her waist, and drew her close. "You don't know how glad I am to be picked on." He took the hunk of fish from her and popped it into his mouth.

"How about we eat and then do a little cloud watching today?"

"Anything you want."

While they ate, Harley would sneak glances at him. He was so tired, and it was all because of her. No one had ever done that before. Well, no one other than her mom or grandma. But Zach had.

Once they were finished, they doused the fire and took their typical cloud watching spot. A steady breeze was blowing, and the tree leaves around them rattled. It kept it from feeling too hot.

They'd barely gotten seated when she twisted in the sand to face him. "Thank you for taking care of me. I've never felt so bad in my life."

"Yeah, I suspect so. You were so hot. I mean, I've taken care of Britney when she was sick, and she's never felt that hot. It felt like you were slipping away there for a little bit."

"Yeah, I think I was."

"I can't say I wasn't scared. At least for a little while. You couldn't breathe. Your temperature would skyrocket again and again," he said and swallowed hard. "You wanted me to tell your mom you loved her." His voice had grown soft.

She didn't remember that. All she remembered was him asking her to stay. "I did?"

Zach scrubbed his face with his hands and said, "Yeah."

Tears pooled in her eyes, and she circled her arms around his neck. "Thank you."

He wrapped his arms around her, resting his head on her shoulder. "I couldn't let you go." His beard tickled her neck as he spoke, and she shivered.

As the silence stretched out, he slowly relaxed against her, sliding down until he was resting in her arms. She combed her fingers through his hair, eliciting a deep breath and a large sigh.

"I'm so tired," he murmured.

"I know. If you don't mind, I'll hold you for a while."

With a small nod of his head and another deep breath, it wasn't long before his chest was rising and falling evenly. She brushed the back of her hand across his cheek and smiled. "You are a sweet, sweet man. And I think you've ruined me."

She was positive he'd taken care of her because he felt like he owed her, but it didn't change how it made her feel about him. She pressed her lips to his forehead and held them there a few heartbeats.

Harley leaned back, studying his face. Her hope was that whoever was searching for them would find them soon. If not, she would be in real trouble. Would be. Already was. "I think I'm going to fall for you, and on the way down, I'm going to break everything. By the time this is over, I'll be in a body cast."

HARLEY RAN her fingers through his hair as his head rested in her lap. They were sitting poolside at a resort. Her long, delicate fingers were soothing. It was a good dream, too. She was next to him, and it made everything right.

Slowly, he opened his eyes, and there she was, combing her fingers through his hair. Now he wished he'd tried to hold on to the dream a little longer because they weren't poolside, and the resort faded as his vision cleared.

Behind her, reds and oranges splashed against the sky as the sun was rising. "I slept all day and through the night?"

"Yeah, you were really tired."

"Wow." He blinked hard. No wonder he felt stiff. "How are you feeling?"

Her lips curved up, and she pulled her hand away from his hair. "I'm better."

He covered his mouth as he yawned, stretched, and rolled onto his side. "That's good."

She hugged him around the neck. "You were so tired yesterday that I'm not sure you heard how grateful I am that you took care of me."

He put his arms around her and tugged her tightly against him. "I like being picked on too much to let anything happen to you."

"You called me mean," she said as she leaned back. She lowered her gaze and then looked at him through a fringe of lashes. It was a jumpstart for his heart. "Are you still going to call me mean?"

"Of course."

Her mouth dropped open. "But you like being picked on."

"Just because I like it doesn't mean I won't tease back."

She rolled her eyes. "Then I'm definitely going to keep picking on you."

Man, he was so glad to see her color back to

normal. To see her smiling and laughing. Those three days where she'd hung on by a thread had been torture. "You have no idea how glad I am to see you feeling better," he said as he pushed her hair over her shoulder.

"I'm sorry I ran off. I promise I won't do it again." She chewed her bottom lip. "I guess I need to—"

He didn't care why. To cut her off, he touched his lips to hers and held them there.

"Zach, I—"

"You said you wished you hadn't stopped me from kissing you," he said and swept his lips across hers. The little shiver it evoked made him smile.

"I don't remember saying that."

He pulled back and locked eyes with her. "Trust me; you did."

It was less than a heartbeat before she held his face and brought his lips to hers. They parted, and he didn't hesitate, slowly deepening the kiss and taking his time to savor her. It'd been so long since he'd kissed someone he had feelings for, and his feelings for Harley went deeper than any he'd ever experienced.

A tiny moan escaped as she threaded her fingers through his hair. It seemed she was as desperate and hungry as he was. He pulled her closer and covered her with his body. She couldn't be close enough, and any amount of space was too much.

Her leg wrapped around his as she took his bottom lip between her teeth. The effect was maddening. A throaty moan came from deep within him. He pinned her arms above her head with one hand and tipped her chin up with his other. He pressed his lips to her neck, and her skin was like satin everywhere he touched. When he'd kissed every inch of her neck, he found her lips again and kissed her like it'd been years since the last.

She broke the kiss and pulled back. "We have things to do this morning."

"I'm perfectly happy with what we're doing."

"I didn't say I wasn't, but we have breakfast to catch, a distress signal to finish, and then—"

He nuzzled her neck with his nose and pressed gentle kisses along her jaw. "I'm not hungry, and I don't want to be found at the moment."

Harley pulled her hands free of his grip and held his face. "You help me get those things done, and—"

"And what?"

"We have time to do other things."

Zach grinned. "Like kissing you?"

"Maybe."

"If that's the case, I need a little more before we do all that work."

She shook her head. "Nope. Work first."

"Then kissing?"

"That depends."

He narrowed his eyes. "On what?"

She quickly pushed him off her and scrambled away. "If you can catch me." Her lips spread into a wide grin, and she put her hands on her hips.

His heart was hammering so hard, he could feel it down to his toes. He smiled in response and pushed off the ground. "Game on." If he needed to catch her, he'd do it.

CHAPTER 17

The game was simple. For every fish he caught on the first try, he got to kiss her. For every one he missed, a point was deducted. If he completely lost, they'd go swimming and he'd get no kisses. Harley wasn't sure who the loser was in that game, but it felt like it was her. Why did she come up with that game again? Because it was fun to watch him grumble.

Zach whirled around and threw the spear.

"That's minus one. You keep going, and you'll be negative."

"You said if I caught you, I got to kiss you. There was no talk of fish being involved."

Harley giggled. "I didn't say how you'd catch me."

"I can't even believe I agreed to this. Why did I let you goad me into this?"

"Cause you're easy?"

He leveled his eyes at her. "You just wait."

"For what?"

"You're going to want me to kiss you, and when I don't, you'll be sorry."

She needed to think about that. The kiss they shared was still giving her goosebumps. It was beyond any kiss she'd ever experienced. Her lips tingled from the memory of his touch, from the way his body felt against her as he covered her. Would he really not kiss her? Was she willing to risk it? "You think so, huh?"

"Yeah, I do."

"Okay, we'll see."

He returned his attention to catching breakfast while she watched. She'd offered to do the work, but he'd insisted. It was fun watching and teasing him. He was just too cute. She kept noticing more and more things about him. How his eyes would crinkle when he was really happy. Or how his lips would pinch together when he was grumpy.

Her heart was on a slippery slope. If she continued to kiss him, there was no way it wouldn't get broken. As she watched him, she smiled.

"I was the one who met Samuel Baldwin at the art

exhibit." The words poured out before she could stop herself.

He locked gazes with her. "I kinda figured that out."

She lowered her gaze to the sand. "On the day we were supposed to get married, he had his driver give me a letter that basically said his father would cut him from the family business if he married me."

"Did he ever call you?"

"No, and when I tried to call him, he wouldn't take my calls." She lifted her gaze to his. "With you being friends with him, I thought if you knew it was me…" She shrugged.

Zach stepped out of the tidal pool and squatted in front of her. "Hey, I'm friends with him like I'm friends with the barista who makes my coffee every morning on the way to work. Sam and I are acquaintances at best, and even if we were friends, it wouldn't change my opinion of you at all."

"It wasn't just that. I'm embarrassed. I wasn't even worth a face-to-face conversation. He just left me there."

He took her hand and held it. "Why would you be embarrassed?"

"I was left at the altar. My family and friends were there."

"He was the jerk. It wasn't your fault."

She lowered her gaze. "I know."

Zach tipped her chin up. "The real question you need to answer is, would you have been happy with him?"

She'd thought about that since they'd crashed. The more she got to know Zach, the clearer the answer became. It wasn't just Zach. It was shoring up enough courage to really look at her relationship with Samuel. "No, not anymore. His family didn't like me, and, quite frankly, I didn't like them."

"Knowing the Baldwins, I can see you not liking them. Did you pick on Sam like you pick on me?"

"No, he'd get really mad. I stopped teasing him when he yelled at me."

"Is that all he did?"

That was all it had taken. When he'd yelled, it was more than just yelling. His face had turned red, contorted, and he'd unleashed a fury on her that she'd never witnessed before. He'd broken a chair against the wall, and it'd scared her. Zach didn't need to know how frightening he was that night. Now, she didn't know why she put up with it. "Yeah."

He narrowed his eyes. "That better be all he did."

"Why? Would you beat 'im up?"

"Absolutely," he said and kissed her.

She playfully smacked him on the arm. "You cheater."

He grinned the most heart-stopping smile imaginable. "Totally worth it," he said as he stood.

"I'm deducting points. You better hope your spearing skills have improved dramatically."

As he stepped into the pool again, he picked up the spear. "Laugh all you want. Tease. I don't care. I've found my motivation."

It was island magic. She knew it was, but it felt good to be wanted by him. The spell would be broken the moment they were found. Until then, she was going to soak him up as much as possible.

HARLEY GRINNED at him from across the spring. He'd never met anyone so fast in his life. That woman could zip around in the water like nobody's business. "When I catch you, I'm going to kiss you for as long as I want."

"*If*. You forgot *if*."

He slowly swam toward her and stopped. This time he was catching her, but he had to be smart about it. The last time he'd tricked her, he'd pretended to hurt his leg. He'd have to use something else this time. The water was too clear to claim something had him.

She lowered herself into the water until just her eyes were showing. He knew she was smiling, because it went all the way to her eyes. A second later, she popped up. "I can't help it that you're bad at spearfishing."

"I should never have agreed to that game. It was a bad game."

"Only because you lost."

"If I recall, you're the one who wished I hadn't stopped kissing you."

Harley chewed her bottom lip as she smiled. "Like I said earlier, I don't remember that."

Oh, he had just the plan. With a kick, he sprinted toward her. He nearly had her, but she slipped from his grip. He tried again, but a little slower. This needed to look real, and not like a fake out. Again, he kicked through the water and stopped. "I need a second."

"You're so faking it."

"No, I don't feel good." He waded out of the water and lay down in the sand with his arm over his eyes.

"Zach?"

"I just need a second."

He heard the slosh of water as she walked out, and he could see her standing just out of reach.

"My gut says you are playing a trick."

Without saying a word, he held his hand up.

She groaned and sat beside him. "I know you're playing. I just know it."

Slowly, he sat up and shook his head. "I hate it when you get that worried tone."

"See, I knew you were pretending."

"I'm not as fast as you." His gaze roamed over her face. "You look tired."

Harley nodded. "I kinda am. I may have done too much with the swimming."

They'd been swimming a few hours, so it wasn't a shock that she felt that way. "You want to go back to camp and rest?"

"No," she said as she pushed him back onto the ground. Heartbeat after heartbeat, she held his gaze as she combed her fingers through his hair. He wished he knew what she was thinking, but he was afraid to break the moment.

She pulled her fingers from his hair, brushing the back of her hand along his cheek. He was finding it harder and harder to breathe. It was so sweet and intimate, like she was trying to memorize his face. She touched her fingertips to his lips with the lightest of caresses and then slowly bent forward, pressing her lips to his.

Zach closed his eyes as she drew her lips across his so delicately it was like a whisper of a kiss. She continued the soft, slow kisses until he was so desperate for more that he slipped his hand into her hair and cupped it to hold her still.

She sucked his bottom lip in between her teeth and then deepened the kiss. It was unhurried, like she was drinking him in. He'd never experienced a kiss like that. One that felt like someone wanted him and only him.

He broke the kiss long enough to roll onto his side and pull her to the ground. She wrapped her arms around his neck, sliding her hands into his hair. He trailed kisses from her lips to her neck, stopping at the hollow of her throat and pressing a soft kiss to her skin.

Harley touched her cheek to his and nuzzled him with her nose. "I—"

"What?"

"I think I hear a helicopter."

They both lay there quietly, listening.

Zach caught her gaze and held it. He wasn't ready to be found. Not yet. He hadn't kissed her as long as he wanted. How could he keep her close until he figured out if he could live without her?

She smiled. "I guess we've been rescued."

The helicopter roared as it set down on the beach, and it felt like the last drop of sand had fallen from the hourglass. His heart dropped to his stomach as she stood.

"We should go."

He pushed off the ground and pulled her to him. "You promised you'd come to the party I'm throwing." It was a lie, but he was desperate.

"No, I didn't."

"When you were sick."

She narrowed her eyes, and as she opened her mouth, their names were called.

"We'll talk later," she said.

He didn't want to talk later. When they got back, there was a possibility she could walk out of his life. She couldn't. Not when he needed more time with her. He'd never felt so desperate in his life. "Harley, promise me you won't disappear."

She pulled free and walked away without saying a word. He'd almost lost her once. Could he handle that again? He needed divine intervention again, or he'd be broken.

CHAPTER 18

The roar of the helicopter couldn't drown out Harley's thoughts. They'd been rescued by the Coast Guard. Matt had called Britney, and when she couldn't get Zach to answer his phone, it was a massive manhunt. They knew Harley was on the plane because of the passenger manifest, which she hadn't thought about.

They'd be stopping in Belize before going back to Houston. The plane had been blown off course, and they'd ended up on an island closer to South America than Jamaica. The crew had missed the wreckage in the surf, and if it weren't for the half-made distress signal, it was possible they'd have flown over them without ever knowing they were there.

Zach had flown into a borderline hurricane that

had quickly formed over the Atlantic. It'd petered out as it reached the Gulf, and by the time it hit land, it was a tropical storm.

With her head against the seat, she stared out the window as the island and its magic faded. Her heart hurt worse than it had ever hurt in her life. One last kiss. That was all she got, and she didn't know how she'd ever move on from Zach.

He'd sounded sincere. Distraught, even, but once they reached civilization, it'd be over. There'd be no more teasing, flirting, or kissing. Their little bubble was popped. In no time, he'd forget her. Tears pooled in her eyes, and she pulled the large blanket the Coast Guard had given her tightly around herself.

Ten days. She'd started the trip determined to hate Zachary Wolf. He was no different from every other rich person she'd ever met. Then she'd gotten to know him, and she'd never been more wrong.

He was a good man. A kind man. He was generous, thoughtful. He'd taken care of her when she'd never felt worse. He was someone she could love until she was old and gray. Oh, it'd be so easy to love him. That heart of his was big and soft and sweet. His smile made her tingle all the way to her toes. The way he'd held her made her feel so wanted. No one would ever be able to hold her like that again.

She thought she'd loved Samuel. Now that she had a comparison, she didn't even know what she'd had with that man. Comparing him to Zach was like comparing dirt to gold. And what she felt for Samuel was a drop in the bucket when she thought about Zach.

Harley looked at him as he sat across from her, slouched in the seat with his eyes closed. Her heart steadily picked up its pace. She'd fallen in love with him. More tears pooled in her eyes, and she pulled her gaze from him. It was just her luck to fall in love with someone who would never feel that way about her.

How had she let herself get so careless? She knew he didn't want a relationship. He'd been upfront and open about it. But there she was, loving him with every inch of her heart.

There was no way she could stay in Houston any longer. If she needed to, she'd stay with her mom until the apartment lease was paid, and then she'd find a place of her own in Lubbock. Her mom had offered once, but Harley had held out hope that she'd find another job.

Houston wasn't the city for her. It was nowhere near big enough when she knew could run into Zach. Plus, he'd want to be nice and try to keep in touch. She didn't want that. Not when she wanted to hold him and kiss him and tell him how much she loved him.

She closed her eyes and wished she'd never boarded that plane. The moment she realized where the job was, she should have done a U-turn and gotten out of there. The ache dug its way a little deeper. For now, she'd let herself grieve, but when they landed, she'd put on a smile and wave goodbye. She could do that until he was out of sight. Then she'd find a big pillow, curl up around it, and cry.

THE ISLAND WAS BARELY OUT of sight when Zach drifted off to sleep. He hadn't wanted to, but the relief of being found coupled with the hum of the helicopter had knocked him out. It hadn't been long, and the short nap had given him more energy.

Zach had flown Harley into a strong tropical storm. The moment he saw the clouds, he should have turned the plane around. He'd been cocky and thought he could handle it. Maybe he should have turned back, but then he wouldn't have had the chance to get to know Harley.

He didn't have long before they would touch down in

Belize, and he needed to come up with a plan to keep Harley around. The desperation he'd felt on the island was nothing compared to what he felt while knowing he was getting closer to her being able to walk out of his life.

He lifted his gaze to her curled-up form in the seat across from him. Her head was leaned back, and her eyes were closed. Even now, he was drawn to her. He didn't even care that he was in a helicopter, surrounded by strangers. If he could, he'd pull her close and kiss her right there in front of everyone.

Didn't that mean something? It had to. He leaned his head back and let his eyes glaze over. What could he do to lengthen his time with her?

Wouldn't they have to stay a night before going to Houston? A doctor would need to see them, right? Maybe he'd have another night to spend with her. To figure out what he wanted and make sure what he was feeling was real.

Or better, Britney.

His heart thrummed as loud as the helicopter. That was it. He knew Britney. She'd want to throw a huge party. Once she found out Harley had worked with Trixie Tanner, there's no way Britney wouldn't be begging Harley to stay and work on the party with her. Not begging, demanding. And his sister was the queen of getting people to what she wanted, most of the time.

Britney, and most likely his mom, would be waiting in Belize to take him back to Houston the moment they touched down. That was his ticket. Britney would love Harley. She'd convince Harley to stay. Maybe even talk her into staying at the house when she found out Harley had literally saved his life twice.

If the Coast Guard crew wouldn't look at him funny, he'd be fist pumping the air. He'd figured out a way to have more time with her. Although, the other side of the coin was Britney suspecting he had feelings for Harley. His sister might be ditzy at times, but she could read him better than anyone.

Once Britney put it together—and she would—he'd be grilled. From both his sister and his mom.

Would his whole family be in town? Zoe, Julian, and Noah? If so, Harley would get to meet them. Then she'd know they were different from the Baldwins.

Hope soared, and his chest tightened. Silently, he prayed his plan would work. At least then, he'd get to thank Harley good and proper for pulling him out of the plane. Maybe planning a party would even open Harley up for jobs so she could stay in Houston.

CHAPTER 19

It was after four in the evening when the jostling of the helicopter setting down jerked Harley awake. She only knew that because the medical team waiting for them told her. It had been less than two weeks, but she understood why they'd need to be checked out. She told them about the sting, but when they checked her leg, they said she was okay. Zach was fine, and they were both encouraged to get rest for the next couple of days.

Two women stood in the distance, and if Harley had to guess, it was Zach's family. It made her wonder where her mom was.

After the medical team was finished, Harley walked with Zach toward them. They didn't get halfway before the two ladies ran to greet them.

"Zach!" the younger one screamed and flew into his arms. "Oh my gosh, I'm so glad you're okay."

The older woman dabbed her eyes and embraced him. "Sweetheart, I haven't had a wink of sleep since you were reported missing."

"I'm fine. I'd like to stay away from seafood for a little while, but other than that, I'm good." He paused a moment and then pressed his palm in the small of Harley's back. "This is Harley Wilson. She saved my life. Harley, this is my sister Britney and my mom, April Wolf."

"Oh, he's being overdramatic. We crashed, and—"

Before Harley could finish, Britney pulled her into a crushing hug, followed by his mom. "I don't know how to thank you."

"It's not a big deal. I should probably go so you guys can spend time with each other."

His mom scoffed and took her hand. "Oh, no, sweetheart, you're with us. I promised your mother I'd take care of you."

"My mom?" Harley smiled.

"When we realized you two were missing, I contacted her. Two mommas with missing kids, well, we were a blubbering mess," his mom said. "I offered to bring her to Houston to stay with us, but she said sitting idle would drive her insane, so she stayed in Lubbock."

That made sense. When her mom was stressed, she had to keep moving. "Yeah, sounds like her."

"I called her when they found you, and she'll be waiting for you at the airport when we arrive in Houston tomorrow."

Zach would get to meet her mom. Why did that make her so happy? "Okay."

April patted her hand and then took Zach's. "We've booked a night at the local resort. We're going to let you two get cleaned up, and then we're going to have something to eat. That way you two can tell us everything."

Zach grinned. "I think they've got the right idea. I'm desperate for a shower."

"And Cocoa Puffs."

"With cold chocolate milk," he said with a chuckle.

Harley laughed.

"And you'll be filling us in on that, too," Britney said.

His mom patted his cheek and hugged him again. He stood there, holding her, and all Harley could think was that it was sweet. She didn't think she could love him more, and then he did that? Man, whatever parts of her heart he hadn't taken up residence in were being filled.

Britney leaned into Harley. "My brother's a momma's boy."

"I heard that," Zach said.

"I said it out loud, so duh."

He caught Harley's gaze, and she smiled. Britney was someone Harley could get along with very well. "You should see him spear fish."

"I'd pay money to see that."

Zach rolled his eyes. "All right, let's go. Harley and I need a shower, clean clothes, and food."

His mom touched Harley's arm. "Tell me what size you wear, and I'll have clothes for you by the time you get out of the shower or bath. Whatever you like."

A bath sounded heavenly. She was sure she had sand embedded in places that weren't decent to speak of. Although, a shower sounded good too. Maybe she could catch a short nap before they ate.

In true billionaire fashion, a limo waited for them, and they were being dropped off at the resort before she could blink. The place was a palace. Harley couldn't believe her eyes. It would take her a lifetime of salary to afford a place like it.

"Uh, this looks really expensive," Harley said.

Zach's mom hooked her arm in Harley's. "Look at me, sweetheart."

Harley met her gaze head-on.

"You're part of this family now. Don't you worry about a thing, okay?"

She chewed her lip.

"She won't take no for an answer, so you may as well just agree," Britney said.

"Okay."

His mom smiled and patted her hand. "Smart girl. Now, let's get you checked in so you can clean up."

It didn't seem that Harley had a choice, and if she was honest with herself, she kind of liked it. Being that welcomed by someone. Zach said his family was great, and he hadn't been exaggerating.

Once they were checked in, Harley found herself in a room that felt too nice to occupy, but the shower was calling her name. She dropped the blanket she'd kept around herself and stepped into the bathroom.

She never thought she'd be so happy to see a toilet. While she undressed, she started the water and then stepped in. Hot water. Soap. Shampoo. Luxuries she'd taken for granted her entire life now held a special meaning to her.

It took six washes for her hair to feel even close to

normal. The water that ran down the drain was murky and gross. When she was finished, she felt like she'd had a film removed from her body. Her skin felt smooth and clean.

She pulled on a towel and stepped out of the bathroom. True to their word, Zach's family had taken her extra room card, and on the bed lay several dresses, jeans, and enough shirts to fill a closet, all of them in colors she would have picked. They'd even managed to find bras and panties for her. Clean underwear was right up there with the toilet in things she never thought she'd be happy to see.

After she was dressed, she tried to find Britney and April, but they weren't in their rooms, so she stopped at Zach's. He opened the door, still looking like he'd been picked up off a deserted island.

"You haven't showered yet?" she asked.

He shook his head and stepped aside so she could enter. "No, I just got off the phone with Matt. He'd made Britney promise that the moment I had the chance, I'd call him to let him know I was all right."

"Oh, I can go so you can clean up."

"You can stay. I'll dress in the bathroom."

"Okay."

He picked up a pair of jeans and a t-shirt. "I'd say I won't be long, but I think I'd be lying."

Harley laughed. "Take your time."

With a smile, he slipped into the bathroom and shut the door. Harley perched on the edge of the bed a moment and then spotted his new suitcase. His family must have brought it for him. She couldn't help but wonder if all he wore was jeans and t-shirts. He'd packed for a working vacation when he was going to Jamaica, so that's all he'd had.

The water started in the bathroom, and she chewed her thumb until her curiosity got the better of her. She slipped off the bed, walked to the suitcase, and peeked inside. A dress shirt and slacks? Huh. As a picture of him wearing them floated to mind, her knees wobbled. No doubt he was downright sexy in that.

She pulled the dress shirt out. It was solid, long-sleeved, and crisp white. It smelled good too. Not soap good, but like it'd been in contact with his cologne. Goodness, is that what he typically smelled like? Thinking back, he *had* smelled amazing when they first met. The ocean, salt, and sand had quickly replaced it, though.

Harley slipped on the shirt. She shouldn't, but after spending almost two weeks with him, she felt lonely when he wasn't around. It hung about as long as his t-shirt. She walked back to the bed, kicked off her shoes, and curled up on the bed.

Wow, it was soft and squishy and comfortable. She wasn't even all that tired until she lay down. The thought hit her that she should take his shirt off before he came out of the bathroom, but it gave her comfort. Maybe she could say she was cold. Before she knew it, her eyes slid shut, and she was out.

WITH HIS HANDS braced against the shower wall, Zach hung his head as the hot water ran down his back. He'd never thought he'd appreciate hot water so much. He didn't realize how disgusting his hair felt until he'd washed it.

Sand-and-grime-filled water ran down the drain the first three times he lathered up. The last time, it finally ran clear and he felt clean. Shaving was the only thing he had left to do, but he'd been unable to pull himself from the water just yet. It felt too good on his muscles. But mostly because Harley had looked so good.

That little yellow spaghetti-strap sundress showed off her soft shoulders and long legs. He'd opened the door for her and nearly drooled. She could look good in anything.

He turned the water off and then shaved. It took forever since it was so long. He'd never liked beards, though he didn't mind the five o'clock shadow. What would Harley like? It didn't hurt to try it out. If she didn't like, he'd shave it off.

Once he was dressed, he stepped out of the bathroom and found Harley asleep in the middle of his bed with his dress shirt on. Why would she have his shirt on? A myriad of reasons floated to mind, but he settled on the thought that maybe she'd been cold.

A soft rap came from the door, and he hurried to answer it. Britney smiled. "Hey!"

"Shhh." He put a finger to his lips and pointed to the bed.

She wrinkled her nose. "Sorry," she said as she walked in. "Mom sent me to get you so we can eat."

"Okay."

She looked over at Harley on the bed. "How can someone that tall sleep all curled-up like that."

"I don't know, but that's the way she sleeps most of the time."

"She has your dress shirt on."

He nodded. "Yeah, I think she was cold."

"Or she wanted to wear your dress shirt."

"Nah." Although, that'd been one of the reasons

he'd considered. He'd spent almost two weeks with her, and it felt weird to be alone now.

Britney tilted her head. "She's so pretty. I've never seen legs so long on a woman. I'm seriously jealous."

"She gorgeous. And sweet, funny, interesting, intelligent, and strong. I've never met a more incredible woman in my life." The words had rolled off his tongue without so much as a hiccup. He squeezed his eyes shut.

His sister gasped. "You're in love with her."

"I don't know."

"Okay, you wake up tomorrow and she's gone. How do you feel?"

She may as well have hit him in the heart with a hammer. "Not good."

"Just *not good*?"

"More like gutted. The whole helicopter ride here, I was trying to think of ways to keep her around."

"Zach, face it. You're in love with her."

Was he? Could he live without her? No. He wanted old and gray, front porch swings and coffee by sunrise with her. His life wasn't worth anything if she wasn't in it. On the island, in Houston, or anywhere else, his feelings for her didn't change. "Yeah, I am. I'm in love with her."

Britney grabbed him in a hug. "I'm so happy for you."

"It's one-sided."

She lifted an eyebrow. "Well, we'll just have to change that. I like her."

"You don't know her."

"I know you, and she'd have to be some kind of special for you to fall in love with her."

"Will you help me?" He could hear the pleading in his voice.

The glint in his sister's eye was almost enough to make him reconsider. "Absolutely."

"I want you to throw a huge party and beg her to help you."

Her eyebrows knitted together. "Beg her? Why?"

"I'll tell you at dinner. Just trust me."

"Okay, you got it. I'll throw a party to end all parties if it means seeing you happy."

He crossed his arms over his chest. "Brit, keep this between us, please? Don't tell Mom yet."

"You know she's going to see it as soon as we sit down to dinner."

"Yeah, but I want to talk to her first. I need to ask her a few things."

His sister's mouth dropped open. "Are you going to talk to Mom about Dad?"

"Yeah. I need to know some things. It would crush me to have what happened to Mom happen to me."

She hugged him again. "You don't know how happy it makes me to hear that."

He returned the hug. "I know."

"Okay, I'll go so you can wake her up. Mom's waiting on us." Britney grinned and spun on her heels.

Zach waited until she was out the door before walking to the bed. He sat on the edge next to Harley and touched her back, gently shaking her. "Hey."

She pushed up and rubbed her eyes. "Wow, I zonked out."

"Are you hungry?"

"Yeah."

He stood and held her hand to help her up. "Were you cold?" he asked, touching his shirt.

Her cheeks bloomed a red so deep they look blistered. Could Britney have been right? "Uh, yeah. But I'm not anymore." She shrugged off the shirt and laid it on the bed as she slipped on her sandals.

Part of him was itching to tease her about blushing, but the other was thrilled he'd managed to see her blush and didn't want to ruin it. "Okay, are you ready, then?"

She nodded and lifted her gaze to his.

Boy, had he fallen. He could stand there looking at

her for the rest of his life. If there was even the slightest chance he could get her to love him back, he was taking it. There'd never be another he would love like he loved her. Now, he just needed to set his plan into motion and see if he could convince her he was worth loving.

CHAPTER 20

The restaurant inside the resort was just as nice as the resort itself. Zach's mom and sister had somehow managed to get them a secluded spot away from the other guests. Not because they were snobs, but because it was a reunion and they wanted to spend some time with Zach.

His mom and sister were some of the sweetest people Harley had ever met. Which explained why Zach was so sweet. They didn't make her feel unwelcome at all. It was a completely different experience from meeting Samuel's family.

They'd ordered several appetizers—nothing seafood—and when it came time to order, Harley had gone with the club sandwich and fries. Her drink never went dry, either.

"Okay, so explain the chocolate milk," Britney said.

Harley giggled. "We were talking about the island being nice if we had little drinks with umbrellas, and it just devolved from there."

"It was torture," Zach said through a laugh. "If this restaurant had Cocoa Puffs, that's what I'd be having."

Britney snorted. "That's still your favorite cereal?"

Zach looked at his sister like that was the craziest question he'd ever heard. "It's chocolate, and it turns the milk chocolate. Of course it's my favorite."

Harley shrugged. "I have to agree with him on that. I mean, cereal is good. Cereal that makes the milk chocolate can't be beat."

"See?" Zach grinned.

"I can see why you survived with him, then," his mom said. "That boy has loved that stuff since he was tiny."

Harley caught his gaze and smiled. He'd shaved the beard but left a little scruff. It was cute, but he looked better without it.

"And what is with that fuzz on your face?" his mom asked.

Had April read her mind?

He shrugged. "I don't know. Thought I'd try something different."

His mom smiled. "Okay, I was just curious."

Britney touched Harley's arm. "How *did* you survive being stuck with him?"

"Oh, it wasn't so bad. He's fun to tease. He pouts."

His mouth dropped open. "I don't pout."

"You do too."

Britney threw her head back and laughed. His mom rolled her lips in.

"I'm being ganged up on," he said.

Harley bumped him with her shoulder. "Wimp."

"Okay, I love you," Britney said.

Zach looked at Harley, and for a heartbeat, he locked eyes with her. Man, those blue eyes of his were sparkling like there was nothing but mischief on his mind. "I told you."

"So, I'm thinking we throw a huge party," Britney said. "Right, Mom?"

April nodded. "You know, I think so. It's not every day you get stranded on a deserted island."

"She was an assistant to Trixie Tanner," Zach said. It hit the conversation like a bomb.

Britney's eyes widened, and her mouth dropped open. "Are you serious? Trixie Tanner?"

"Um, yeah."

"Oh, then you're staying at the house. You have to. I'm good at planning, but I'm not Trixie-Tanner-assistant good."

Harley's cheeks heated. "Uh."

Britney's shoulders sagged. "Please?" That girl could work the sad puppy eyes. How was she still single?

"I don't know. My mom—"

"Will stay too," April said. "I wanted to meet her in person anyway."

Harley suddenly felt like she was the one being ganged up on. "You're not taking no for an answer, are you?"

Britney grinned. "Nope." She touched Harley's arm. "You saved my brother's life. I think that deserves a party."

"How *did* she save you, Zach?" asked April.

Zach glanced at Harley. "I'd hit my head. If she hadn't pulled me out, I would've drowned."

His mom's eyes glistened. "I see." Her voice was so soft. "Well, then that certainly does deserve a party."

"That's not the only time. There was a waterfall on the island. We were standing on the ledge, looking at it. The ground gave way, and she pulled me back. If I'd fallen, I wouldn't be here."

Harley's cheeks heated again. He'd taken care of her too. It wasn't like she'd been the lone rescuer. They'd taken care of each other. "Yeah, but that was easy stuff. I was stung by something bad. I don't know what, but I'm pretty sure I would've died if he hadn't taken care of me. So, I'm thinking we're even. That's if we're keeping score, which I'm not."

"That sounds terrifying," his mom said.

Zach cleared his throat. "Yeah, it was."

"Okay, that settles it. You're staying with us until the party. Right, Mom?" Britney smiled.

April nodded. "Yeah, that's my vote."

Britney shrugged. "See, you're outnumbered."

"All right." It made her feel so good to be liked by his family, but it made her sad too. She really liked his mom and sister.

His sister clapped. "Yay. This will be so fun."

Britney's sincerity was infectious. Harley found herself looking forward to spending time with her. Until she realized she'd be spending time with Zach too. How much harder would it be to leave when she'd fallen in love with his whole family?

Zach leaned in and put his lips to her ear. "I do believe 'I told you so' works in this situation."

When he pulled back, he shot her a smile that made him as kissable as he'd ever been. If his mom and sister weren't sitting at the table, she could say with certainty that she'd be doing just that. No, she couldn't, no matter how much she wanted to. He didn't want a relationship, and those kisses on the island didn't mean anything.

Her chest tightened. She needed to help Britney get the party planned and then get away from him. It was already going to hurt, but if she got any more attached, she'd be broken forever.

BRITNEY HAD DONE IT. He'd never be able to thank her enough. Harley was staying until the party. He wasn't sure how long it'd take them to pull it together, but it'd be at least another day. It was one more day than he had when they sat down to eat.

"I forgot to ask you, Harley, did you like the clothes we picked out?" his mom asked.

She touched her dress. "I loved them. Yellow is my favorite color."

His mom smiled. "I thought you'd look beautiful in it. I was right."

Harley's cheeks turned bright red again, and the color went all the way to her ears. "Thank you."

Britney leaned forward with her arms on the table. "So, start from the beginning. What happened?"

They took turns telling his mom and sister the details, minus the part where he kissed her. Harley took pleasure in telling them about his fishing in excruciating detail. He didn't think his mom could laugh so loud.

"It's not that funny," Zach said.

His sister cackled. "It's hysterical."

"I have to agree with her," his mom said. "You were never one to take failing well."

Harley touched his hand. "Actually, he didn't do too bad. After that first time, he was okay. Slow, but he got better every time. He learned how to make fire pretty quickly too."

"She's being nice on that last one."

"I'm not." Harley locked eyes with him and smiled. "I was proud of you."

Heat rushed to his cheeks. She'd tongue-tied him in front of his mom and sister.

"You two sound like you worked well together," his mom said. When she caught Zach's gaze, an unspoken understanding passed between them. They'd be talking when they got home. Britney was right. His mom knew exactly how he felt about Harley.

They talked a little longer, and once they'd finished their meal, they went to their rooms. Zach walked Harley to hers, and the temptation to kiss her was so strong it felt more like an ache that couldn't be satisfied. He somehow contained it, though.

He'd been exhausted at dinner, but once he reached his room and lay down, he was restless. All he could think about were the coming days. Trying to convince Harley that he'd been wrong about not having a relationship. That he'd fallen in love with her because of her, not because she'd saved him. That he loved her, no matter where they were.

A soft knock came from the door, and he swung his legs over the bed and stood. He opened the door, and his pulse jumped. Harley stood there in a cute little t-shirt and shorts. Her skin couldn't look softer.

"I'm sorry. I shouldn't have…"

He took her by the elbow and pulled her in. "It's okay. I can't sleep."

"Me either. I'm exhausted, but I can't stop tossing and turning," she said as she crossed the room and sat in one of the chairs by the window.

"You too? What's keeping you awake?"

She tucked a piece of hair behind her ear. "I don't know. I just can't."

Zach had a feeling that wasn't the whole story, but it wasn't like he was willing to tell her why he was still awake either. He wanted her to stay. Maybe if she was close, he could get to sleep. "We could find a movie. Watch it until we fall asleep."

"Okay."

They stuffed pillows against the headboard and crawled onto the bed. Zach flipped the television on and surfed channels for a bit. "Oh, hey, *Galaxy Quest*."

"I'm good with that. I love that movie."

"You do?" he asked. "I'm always the only who loves that movie."

She smiled. "Yeah, I really do."

He set the remote down and let the movie play.

She stared at him without saying a word, like she was debating something in her mind.

"What?" he asked.

"Keeping the scruff, huh?"

"I don't know. Like I said, I'm just trying it out. You don't like it?"

"It's your face. Do you like it?"

He shrugged. "It's okay. Kind of itchy." Actually, he hated it. He'd keep it if she liked it, but otherwise, it'd be gone.

"I think you look good with or without it."

"You think I look good, do you?" He wiggled his eyebrows.

She leveled her eyes at him. "You know what I mean."

"If you had a vote, which would it be? Shave or not?"

"Shave."

He nearly cheered. It'd be gone first thing in the morning. "I'll take that into consideration."

Harley sank further down into the bed. "It feels weird to be back around people. We weren't even gone that long."

"Yeah, I know what you mean."

"And I've always had a hard time getting to sleep in strange places."

"Is that why you came to me?"

"Maybe."

Zach slipped his arm around her and pulled her to him. "Better?"

She stretched her arm over his chest and laid her head on his shoulder. "Much."

"Glad to be of service." And ecstatic that he had her close. Maybe he'd sleep now too. He combed his fingers down the length of her hair, and she moaned as she melted into him. It only took a few more times before she was breathing evenly.

This was what he wanted every night. He wanted to go to sleep with Harley next to him. Her face being the last thing he saw at night and the first thing he saw in the morning. Being with her would work.

It meant he'd have to find people to trust to run the company. He wouldn't be spending every minute there. If Harley was in his life, he'd be balancing things. He'd be spending time with her. They'd be having dinner together, spending the evening talking, or like this, watching a movie cuddled together.

Being with her would be worth whatever trials came. He didn't think things would be perfect, but they'd be worth fighting for because he loved her, and he wanted to be loved by her.

CHAPTER 21

Waking up in Zach's arms was the best part of Harley's morning. On one hand, it made her a little giddy to have been close to him all night and to wake up to him. He was beautiful. On the other, it was painful to know it would soon come to an end.

His mom and sister were being kind, but he'd told them she'd saved his life. How else were they supposed to be? Harley suspected that if it was her child that had been saved from drowning, she'd be a little sentimental and sweet to the person who'd rescued them.

She'd left him sleeping and went back to her room to get ready for their flight later. The prospect of seeing her mom had her anxious to get to Houston.

Then she had a huge party to plan. That made her a little nervous too. Would the Baldwins be invited?

A knock came from the door, and Harley answered it. "Hey, Britney."

Zach's sister stood at her door with a suitcase. "It occurred to me that you didn't have a suitcase for your clothes, so I got you one."

Harley waved her in. "Thank you. You didn't have to do that."

"Well, seeing as everything you had is on that island or in the ocean somewhere, yeah, I kinda did." She laughed.

"I appreciate it. You and your mom have been so gracious. I can't thank you enough for the room and the clothes. It was so nice of you."

"You're welcome. We're getting ready, and we're planning to meet in the lobby. We thought we'd grab a quick bite for breakfast before getting on the plane."

"Okay."

"We'll see you down there," Britney said as she walked away.

Harley took a deep breath and shut the door before stepping into the bathroom.

Once she was dressed, she met Zach and his family in the lobby. After they ate, they boarded a second plane that Zach's father had owned. Air travel on private planes was so much different from public.

When the plane touched down, Harley could see her mom standing by a waiting limo. Harley's whole body was shaking by the time her feet hit the last stair.

Her mom squealed and ran toward her. She grabbed Harley in a hug and swayed back and forth. "Oh, honey, I'm so glad to see you. I haven't cried so much in my life."

Harley dropped her luggage and returned her mom's hug. "I'm okay. I'm sorry you were worried."

"I'm just glad to have you back."

Zach's family stopped a few feet away. Harley waved at them to come closer. "This is Zach, his sister Britney, and his mom—"

"April." Her mom hugged Zach's mom like they were old friends. "I'm so glad to meet you."

"Penny, I've been so looking forward to meeting you. I'm so sorry about all of this."

"We've got them back. That's all that matters."

April hugged Zach around the waist. "So true. And I can't tell you how thankful I am for Harley. Zach said she saved his life. He would have drowned if it wasn't for her."

Harley's cheeks went from fine to flaming in the

blink of an eye. Why couldn't they stop bringing that up? "If I hadn't saved him, it would've been boring, so it was for selfish reasons."

Zach chuckled. "I'm glad you had selfish reasons, then."

"Me too," Britney said.

Zach's mom clapped her hands together. "Well, why don't we finish this at the house? Zoe, Julian, and Noah are all waiting for us."

"They are?" Zach asked.

"Yeah, sweetheart. They'd have flown with me, but they loved me enough to let me have a moment with you first. Britney, of course, was coming with me."

"Of course," Zach said and smiled.

Britney rolled her eyes. "Shut up."

"Well, I can't wait to meet them," Harley's mom said. "And I can't wait to chat with you over a cup of coffee."

"And coffee cake," Zach's mom said.

"Oh, honey, yes. I'm down for cake all the time."

April chuckled. "Oh, me too."

Harley smiled at the thought of meeting the rest of his family. If they were as great as his mom and sister, she had no doubt it'd be wonderful to get to know them. She was curious how they treated Zach. Would they tease him as much as Britney did?

A few more days. Maybe. She had no idea how quickly Britney could pull a party together. At least, putting a party together would give Harley something to do. Plus, it would be a good way to get her feet wet again. When she returned to Lubbock, she could start her party planning business and give herself something to do while she got over Zach.

THE FLIGHT HOME was what could best be described as boring and uneventful, other than the occasional joke at Zach's expense, which Britney and Harley seemed to love. Though, he did have to admit he loved hearing Harley laugh. He could picture that sound filling his home, and it made him that much more determined to get her to believe him when he finally told her he loved her.

He walked through the front door of his family home, and Zoe, Julian, and Noah were waiting for him. They greeted him with hugs and smiles. When he'd left, he hadn't realized how pregnant Zoe was and just what a glow it gave her.

"Oh, Zach," she said as she hugged him, her belly making it awkward. She held him a few moments before leaning back. "I've never been so happy to see that mug of yours."

"I'm glad to be home."

Julian shook his hand and pulled him into a hug. "Man, you had us worried."

"Yeah, that was tense," Noah said.

Zach stepped back and palmed the small of Harley's back to guide her forward. "This is Harley Wilson."

"Wow. Are you sure you didn't strand yourself on purpose?" Noah asked.

Harley's cheeks flashed red. "Hi. It's nice to meet you all."

Julian shook her hand. "It's nice to meet you. I think Noah might be on to something."

"Shut up," Zach said. His own cheeks were beginning to feel like they were on fire.

Zoe grinned. "Oh, you made him blush."

"And suddenly, I wish the three of you would have just called." He paused. "Besides, you're keeping me from introducing her mother. This is Penny Wilson."

They each greeted her mom, and then the hugs were flying between them and Britney and his mom. Once the hugs and welcomes were done, his mom showed Harley and her mom where they'd be staying. He didn't know if it was coincidence or not, but

Harley was put across the hall from him. Either way, he wasn't complaining. Maybe he could steal a kiss later. Couldn't hurt to try, right?

It felt strange to be standing in his childhood room. Not twenty-four hours ago, he was on an uninhabited island. Not that he was complaining. It was just an odd feeling.

His door cracked open. "Zach, may I come in?" his mom asked.

Well, he knew she'd want to talk when they got home. He just didn't think it'd be this quick. "Sure."

She slipped inside and shut the door. "Britney said you needed to speak with me, and since we haven't really talked in a while, I was hoping that meant something."

He turned from the window. "He was sick, wasn't he?"

"Yeah, sweetheart, he was sick."

"With what?"

His mom walked to the bed and sat. "He'd been having headaches, and I convinced him to see a doctor. They ran a few tests and did a brain scan."

Zach's chest tightened. "Okay."

"He had a tumor in the section of his brain that controls behavior and personality."

"When did you find this out?"

"You'd just started college."

"Why didn't you tell me then?"

His mom folded her hands in her lap. "We talked about that. He wanted you to go to college and not worry about him. He didn't want you to feel obligated to come home. You needed to spread your wings."

"It should have been my decision."

"Honey, do you remember when things started getting really bad? When your dad was at his cruelest? I tried to talk to you."

Zach lowered his gaze. He remembered. At the time, he was so self-centered that he wasn't interested in anything to do with his family. "Yeah. I didn't want to. I didn't care."

"And I didn't and don't hold it against you. You were young, just out on your own, and experiencing life." She paused. "Your dad loved you so much, and he was so proud of you."

"But you'd cry and look so hurt. He was divorcing you."

"Because at the end, he wasn't the man I'd fallen in love with, but he couldn't help it. That's why you'd find me crying. The man I loved was in there somewhere, and this thing was eating him alive. There was —" she said and stopped as her voice cracked. "There was nothing I could do. He protected me, though. He didn't change the will to cut me out because he couldn't, and he couldn't divorce me. He'd made arrangements with an attorney. In the event of his behavior growing out of control, he wouldn't be allowed to change it. I was given custody of him."

Zach covered his mouth with his hand. It felt like weights were being set on his chest. "So, all those times he was cruel to you?"

"He couldn't help it. None of it."

He walked to the bed and sat beside his mom. "I'm so sorry."

"I think you knew deep down what was happening, and distancing yourself was the way you chose to handle it. We all had our ways of coping, and I understood."

He put his arm around her. "I'm sorry, Mom. I should have been willing to listen sooner."

"Maybe, but maybe the timing is just right. That lovely young woman across the hall may not be there if you'd done anything differently." She smiled. "I see the way you look at her."

His cheeks burned. "Mom."

"You're in love with her. I saw the way your eyes sparkled when you looked at her. The flush in your cheeks."

"Yeah, I am."

"Are you going to tell her?"

"I want to, but…I told her…I don't want to have a relationship."

His mom grinned, and after a long pause, she said, "You're afraid."

"What if she doesn't love me back?"

"Honey, love is a risk. It's not easy or predictable, but even if I'd known what would happen to your dad, I'd do it again. His love was worth *every* tear I shed. Is she worth it?"

Zach nodded and didn't even hesitate with the answer. "She's worth everything."

"Then go for it. I'm not saying you'll get what you want, but you won't get anything if you don't try."

"Yes, ma'am."

She hugged him. "I'm so glad to have you home, sweetheart."

"I'm glad to be home, and thanks for putting up with me."

His mom leaned back. "You've been worth every tear too." She patted his leg and stood. "We're all having dinner together in a little while, okay?"

"Yes, ma'am."

She walked to the door, and with her hand on the knob, she paused. "For what it's worth, I like her and her mom. I'm not opposed to calling either of them family." She winked, opened the door, and walked out.

Zach chuckled. "Real subtle, Mom."

CHAPTER 22

Dinner with Zach's family was a riot. His brothers were merciless, and Harley laughed until she hurt. He was so red-faced by the end, she expected smoke to start pouring out of his ears.

When dinner was over, Zach asked if she'd take a walk with him. Like she'd say no to spending time alone with him. She'd been desperate for a moment alone with him, even after overhearing him tell his mom he didn't want a relationship. It wasn't like she didn't know that, but, boy, it'd stung…again. She'd quickly slipped back into her room and shed more tears than she was comfortable admitting.

"And you thought I was mean," Harley said as she sat with him under a tree.

"Noah is a jerk."

"Yeah, but he sure is cute."

Zach cut a look to her that could've melted concrete. "He's not cute."

"Yes, he is. You just don't like that he picked on you and you can't tickle him."

"No, but I could deck him."

She bumped him with her shoulder. "Grouch."

"I'm not."

"Are too, but you're cute when you're grouchy."

He shot her a brilliant smile. "I'm cute, huh?"

"I think that was established on the island."

"Do you still feel strange?"

Harley nodded. "Yeah, I can't shake the weird feeling yet. Then again, nothing's been normal yet."

"No, I guess not." He paused, and a pained expression crossed his features.

"Are you okay?"

He shrugged. "I don't know. I talked to my mom about my dad. About why he was so different at the end."

"What'd she say?"

"He had a brain tumor."

She gasped and put her hand to her mouth. "Oh, Zach, I'm so sorry."

"Yeah," he said, barely above a whisper.

Harley twisted in the grass and circled her arms around his neck.

"I didn't even give her the opportunity to explain. I just shut her down every time. I was so angry and hurt. And I can't stop thinking that maybe if I'd been a better person, things would have been easier for her."

She squeezed him harder.

He wrapped his arms around her and buried his face in her neck. "I feel so lousy." His voice broke, and the last word came out like a choke. "All through dinner, I tried to just tell myself it was the past, but he was my dad. I didn't extend any grace or mercy to the man." He pulled back. "My dad was a good man. He treated us like we were his world. And when bad times hit, I just wrote him off." A tear streaked down his cheek, and he swiped it off.

The pure grief pouring off him made her want to kiss all his hurt away. She held his face and kissed his forehead. "You are a good person, Zach. He was someone you loved, and I bet you knew something was wrong. It was your way of dealing with what was happening. It hurt to watch your dad become someone you didn't know, and it was your way of protecting yourself."

"That's the problem. I should have been man enough to face it. He was my *dad*. I didn't even...I didn't even say goodbye to him before he died." He lowered his gaze, and his body shook.

Harley hugged him around the neck again, and he pulled her into a crushing embrace as he wept bitter tears. Her heart broke for him. What could she say? How could she ease his hurt? "I have no doubt he knew you loved him. After meeting your family, I see your dad's love in every one of you. I know he was a good man, because you're a good man." She kissed the side of his face and held him tighter.

She knew Zach was a good man. If he wasn't, learning what happened to his dad wouldn't be hitting him so hard. Zach had such a sweet heart, and she loved him so much. If she could, she'd hold on to him forever and never let him go.

When he finally pulled back, he kept his gaze lowered. "I'm sorry. I took what was supposed to be a light, fun evening and turned it into—"

Harley tipped his chin up with one finger. "No, there's nothing to be sorry for. You were hurting. It's okay."

"Harley, if I asked you to kiss me, would you?"

Would she? She sure wanted to kiss him, but she wanted so much more. All of her wanted all of him. If she kissed him, it would hurt like being cut with a thousand knives, because she knew she couldn't have him. He didn't want all of her.

"It's okay. It was stupid to ask," he said, pulling his face away from her.

Oh, it would make her ache to kiss him and know she couldn't have more, but she loved him, and he needed her. Didn't loving someone mean you were there when they needed you?

This wasn't just a simple kiss, though. He was desperate to soothe an ache, and she understood that. If that's what he wanted, that's what she'd give him. Holding his gaze, she pushed him back into the grass. She smoothed his hair back and brushed the back of her hand against his cheek before bending down to sweep her parted lips across his.

The second her lips touched his skin, it was like a fever hit her. All rational thought was gone, and all she could think was that she couldn't get enough of him. Her skin tingled, her senses felt overloaded, and goosebumps marched like Army soldiers down her spine. She brushed her lips across his cheeks, down his jaw, and along his neck before bringing them back to his lips and hovering over them.

Their breath mingled as she held her lips away from his. She sucked his bottom lip between her lips and pulled on it before letting it go and hovering a breath away again. He lifted his head, trying to kiss her, and she pulled back a fraction. She teased his lips again, and when he tried to kiss her, she moved just out of reach.

He groaned as he opened his eyes. "Harley, please."

As a response to his pleading, she brought her lips down to his and deepened the kiss.

The deep, throaty moan that came from him sent a shiver through her. He buried his hands in her hair as the kiss intensified.

Harley felt like her lungs were going to pop from lack of oxygen, but with every touch of his lips, she only wanted more.

Zach broke the kiss, and his chest heaved in and out. He touched his forehead to hers and kept it there until his breathing slowed. "I know I said I didn't want a relationship—"

Harley put her fingers to his lips and pulled back. She'd heard him say it, and she didn't want him to promise something she knew he couldn't deliver or to try to change for her. It wouldn't work. "Don't. This is okay the way it is."

"But—"

"No," she said and kissed him. Then she pushed off the ground. "This wouldn't work. It'd be broken before we started." Before he could protest, she turned and quickly walked away. She knew kissing would him would break her, but she'd had no idea that it would completely shatter her.

She walked to her room, closed the door, and curled up on the bed. Tears trickled down her cheeks. Zach was a good man. So good that he felt obligated to try to change for her. That wasn't something she could stomach. How long would it take before he hated and resented her? She'd rather have a moment with him that was sweet and wonderful than years that ended with him hating her.

Only, it didn't make it hurt any less. She'd kissed him, trying to ease his pain, but who was going to ease hers?

MIND-BLOWING. The kiss Harley had laid on him had been out of this world, mind-blowing. Zach had never wanted someone so much in his life. When he'd asked, he'd never expected to have his socks blown to another country.

Just thinking about it sent sparks of electricity through him. He was almost tempted to walk across the hall at—he looked at the time on his phone—three in the morning to ask for another. Although, a kiss like that in private wouldn't remain just a kiss. Not with Harley.

She wouldn't even hear him out. He hadn't wanted a relationship until he met her. Now he wanted more than a relationship. He wanted forever with rings and vows and pledges of undying love. Tomorrow, if it was possible.

He tried to remind himself that he'd only known her twelve days, but it didn't matter. She was the one. All this time, his heart had been waiting for her. He didn't want anyone else and couldn't fathom a second without being with her.

Zach sat up in the bed and swung his legs over the side. Lying in bed was doing nothing but driving him insane. And if he stayed there much longer, he'd be giving in to temptation and knocking on Harley's door.

With a sigh of frustration, he stood and made his way down to the kitchen. He startled as he found Julian and Noah at the bar with drinks in front of them.

"Hey, Zach," Julian said. "What's kept you up?"

"Nothing," he said.

Noah lifted an eyebrow. "Oh, I'm guessing it was that kiss with the beautiful woman that has him looking so frazzled."

"Shut up, Noah," Zach said.

Julian chuckled. "That has my vote too."

"What? Were you spying on me?" Zach asked.

"Yes," they both said at the same time.

Zach flopped down onto a barstool and grumbled, "I hate both of you."

"But you love her," Noah said.

"I don't want to talk about this with the two of you. You're both jerks."

Julian stood, pulled a scotch glass out, and poured a generous amount of amber liquid in it. "We're jerks, but we love you. Talk," he said, taking a seat next to Zach.

Zach picked up the glass and tipped it up, letting the liquid burn a trail to his stomach. He set the glass down, trying to decide if he wanted to discuss it with his brothers.

"She is hot," Noah said.

Julian snorted. "She has legs that don't stop."

"If you two keep going, I'm going to pound you. Don't talk about her legs or any of her other parts."

Noah and Julian laughed. "We're just giving you a hard time. It's our job," Noah said.

"I hate talking about this stuff," Zach said and drained his glass.

Julian put a hand on his shoulder. "Zach, if you love

her, don't let her go." The way his brother said it made him wonder if Julian's relationship had soured.

"You've got experience with that?" Zach asked Julian.

His brother dropped his hand and looked away. "We aren't talking about me."

"We could be," Zach said and grinned.

Julian punched him on the arm. "No, we couldn't." There was an edge to his voice that held a warning.

Zach caught Noah's gaze and lifted an eyebrow. He gave a slight shake of his head. Whatever it was, it wasn't good. That kind of tone wasn't normal for Julian.

Noah leaned against the island bar. "So, you fell in love with her. Tell her and be done with it."

"It's not that simple. I told her I didn't want a relationship. Now, she thinks the only reason I want to be with her is because she saved my life."

Noah nodded. "Brit told us what she did. It'd be hard not to have feelings for her."

"My feelings have nothing to do with that. She is the easiest woman to love," Zach replied. "She doesn't treat me like I'm someone to use. She's funny, kind, and intelligent. You don't understand. There'll never be another like her."

"Then it sounds like you need to convince her of that," Julian said.

Zach raked his hand through his hair. "I tried. She won't even hear me out."

Noah shook his head. "So, that's it, then?"

"I don't know what to do. I tried to tell her tonight, and it was the same thing. What can I do?"

Julian chuckled. "Take away her chance to speak. We're having a party. Make it a formal declaration in front of everyone."

Something about that didn't set right in Zach's gut. His feelings for Harley weren't some generic thing. "No, she needs to hear me. It needs to be the two of us, sitting alone, and me telling her what she means to me. Telling her in front of people feels wrong." It also sounded like something Sam would do, and if Sam did it, Zach wanted no part of it.

"Then...show her. Not over the top, crazy displays. Something she'd love. Something that will *make* her listen," Julian said.

What could he do to make her listen? "What?"

Noah grinned. "Why don't you try dating her? That's usually a good way to tell a woman you want to be with her."

Date her? Oh man, how long had it been since he dated? "Like dinner or something?"

"Just how long has it been since you've dated a woman?" Noah asked.

"Shut up," Zach said.

Julian snorted. "He has a point, Zach."

"You shut up, too," he said. Julian and Noah did have a point. He could plan a date, right? Take her to a great restaurant…No, take her somewhere regular. Sam would have done over-the-top stupid things. He wasn't Sam, and he didn't want her to think he was trying to be like Sam.

Well, there went the rest of his night. He'd be up, trying to plan the perfect date. Something she'd love that would show her he wanted more. Then she'd have to listen, right?

Julian punched Zach in the shoulder. "I've seen that look before."

Noah chuckled. "Yep, he's got on his thinking face."

Zach stood. "I'm going to bed. I'll see you two later." He walked off with the thought of a nice meal or some Cocoa Puffs and time with Harley without the prying eyes and ears of his siblings. Hopefully, he didn't screw it up. He needed her, and she needed to know it.

CHAPTER 23

"Well, that'll teach her," Britney said as they exited Elise's Bakery. "You don't say no to me, and she better never say no to you ever again."

Harley was in awe. Earlier that morning, she'd called the bakery to set up the catering, and Elise Jacobs had hung up on her. Harley knew the woman. It was because of Harley that Elise's Bakery was on the map. And she wouldn't even speak to Harley. "I don't know what happened. It's like someone has labeled me with a big red X."

Britney squared her shoulders. "I don't know either, but we'll set them straight. Just watch."

From the bakery, they walked to a company that could provide a cereal bar. Harley's idea was to have all sorts of cereals available. It'd be funny to watch women in thousand-dollar gowns trying to chow down on cereal.

After Elise wouldn't speak to Harley, Britney decided that face-to-face meetings were in order at each business. The door chimed as they walked in, and Nathan Kingsley looked up. A look of shock registered on his face. "Harley, I can't help you."

"Why? What have I done? I was the contact person when we used you for Cara Rogers' thirteenth birthday party. You didn't have a problem with me then."

Britney crossed her arms and leaned back. "My name is Britney Wolf. Harley Wilson is my friend."

Nathan's face paled. "Wolf, as in—"

"The Wolf billionaires. I hate slinging that word around, but it seems I have to. Now, you're the second person today that's told my friend they can't work with her. I'm going to ask you what's going on, and you're going to tell me, or you won't have a business when I get done telling all my other friends." Britney's lips formed a thin line, and she didn't break eye contact.

Harley didn't want to ever get on her bad side. "I'd kind of like to know what happened too."

Nathan cursed under his breath. "Trixie said you

were blacklisted. If I did any business with you, she wouldn't use me anymore."

Tears pricked Harley's eyes. "Trixie? Why?" What had Harley done that would cause Trixie to do that to her?

Britney cocked an eyebrow. "Oh, really? Well, let it hereby be known that she's un-blacklisted. And if Trixie wants to work in Houston anymore, she needs clear up this misunderstanding."

"But…You don't understand. Trixie has clout with vendors, other planners, and influential people. If I go against her, I could go out of business," Nathan said.

"Fine, you're working for me, then. I'll take care of Trixie personally," Britney said. "Now, here's what I need."

Once Britney gave Nathan the details of the party and what she wanted, they walked out of the shop. Harley leaned against the brick wall just outside. Her head was spinning. "I don't know what I could've done, Britney. I thought I was good at my job. When she fired me, she didn't tell me why, but I didn't think it was so bad she'd blacklist me."

Britney took her by the shoulders. "Don't worry, Harley. I'm going to find out what's going on. We're family, and we stick together."

It was sweet of her to say that. "I appreciate that, but I don't want my problems to become yours."

"Harley, I like you. I hope to have you around long enough to be best friends. I don't consider your problems to be problems. Just questions that need answers." Britney pulled her into a hug.

Harley returned the hug. "Thank you."

She leaned back. "Okay, now that that's taken care of, dresses. We need fabulous dresses."

How did Harley tell her she didn't have the money for a dress?

"I see that look in your eyes. Don't worry about it. Mom said to take you and to pick out whatever dresses we want. She's going to lunch with your mom, and they're doing the same thing." Britney hooked her arm in Harley's and pulled her from the wall. "Come on, let's find dresses that will make the men cry."

Harley laughed. The more time she spent with Britney, the more she loved her. Talk about a great sister. She was so funny and feisty and friendly. "Okay."

They walked three blocks to a little boutique with dresses that looked expensive enough to pay two months' rent at her current apartment. They tried on dress after dress, finally giving up and walking a block to another store.

"Oh, Britney, I don't know," Harley said as she turned one way then the other as she looked at herself in the mirror. "It's so tight."

Britney smoothed down the front of the black organza gown she was trying. "I think that's the men crying part." She smiled. "And it's not that tight. It's flattering."

"It's short too."

"Again, men crying. I'm so jealous of your legs."

Harley wrinkled her nose. "What?"

Britney snorted. "Oh please. You have legs to die for. They're so long. I'm five feet in heels on a good day. I'm jealous."

"I don't know."

"Zach would love it."

He would? Suddenly, the dress fit just right. If he'd love it, that was good, right?

"He's fallen in love with you," Britney said.

If only. "No, I saved his life. That's all he's feeling."

"No, he's not. My brother hasn't even looked at a girl in years, and I can see it when he looks at you. He's totally in love with you."

Harley had heard what he told April. He didn't want a relationship. No matter what Britney might think, he wasn't in love with her. Maybe infatuation, but Harley wanted more than that. "No, he's not."

Britney tilted her head as she turned to Harley. "Why do you say that?"

"I overheard him talking to your mom the first night here. He said he doesn't want a relationship."

Her eyebrows pulled together like she was trying to digest what Harley had just said. "Are you sure that's what you heard?"

"Positive. Britney, I think he's wonderful, but someone who doesn't want a relationship can't be forced into one. It won't work."

"I just have a hard time believing he said it," Britney said and faced the mirror. "You love him, don't you?"

Harley smiled and lowered her gaze. "We were stranded together for almost two weeks. I care about him, but it's best if I don't go down that road."

"But—"

"Let's just have fun, okay?"

Britney nodded, but she kept the confused look on her face. "Right. Well, I think this is the one for me. How about you?"

"I think this one is for me too. It's shorter than I normally go for, but it's a celebration, right?"

Zach's sister brightened. "Exactly."

Harley chewed her lip and looked over the dress once more. Why did she feel like she needed permission from her mom to wear it?

The sun inched behind the trees as Zach sat on the veranda overlooking the backyard. The tea-filled glass sitting on the table was ringed with condensation as the heat melted the ice.

He'd planned to ask Harley out, but they were gone by the time he crawled out of bed. That's what he got for staying up more than half the night.

"Hello, big brother. I thought you would've had enough sun to last you a while," Britney said as she walked onto the patio with Harley in tow.

"I just needed something to do," he said. "Where have you two been?"

"We needed to talk to a couple of vendors about the party tomorrow and find dresses." Britney smiled and then cast a glance at Harley. "Wait until you see hers."

Zach smiled. "I bet it looks great. Uh, Harley, I was wondering if you'd want to go out tonight? You know, to dinner with me?"

"Uh, I'm sorry. I can't." She lowered her gaze. "My mom and I planned to spend some time together tonight."

With the way Harley was avoiding eye contact, he was struggling to believe her excuse. "Oh.

Okay." Maybe she just didn't want to go out with him.

"I think I'll go put up my dress and see if my mom is back," Harley said. "I had a great time today, Britney. Thank you so much for your help."

His sister smiled and gave her a one-arm hug. "It was a lot of fun, and we'll have to do it again."

Harley returned her smile and walked back into the house. The moment she was out of earshot, Britney sat down. "Did you tell Mom you didn't want to be in a relationship with Harley?"

"What? No. Where'd you get that?"

"Harley."

"Harley? What?" His voice rose an octave.

Britney leaned forward. "Harley said she overheard you telling Mom you didn't want to have a relationship. She swears up and down that's what she heard."

Zach felt like his heart had been trampled. "I said that, but she didn't hear the whole conversation." He hung his head. "That's why she took off last night."

"You mean after that I-need-a-cold-shower kiss you had?"

His face fell. "Did all of you see that?"

Her lips quirked up. "Uh, yeah. You were making out in full view of the window. Of course we saw it."

"Mom?"

"Are you kidding? She's the one who called us over."

His cheeks heated, and he put his head in his hands. "I'm never going to live that down, am I?"

"No, probably not."

Zach groaned. "I hate all of you."

"Back to the problem at hand. What *whole* conversation could you have been having that included a sentence about you not wanting a relationship?"

He lifted his head. "I was telling Mom about wanting to tell her I loved her but that I'd made the stupid mistake of saying I didn't want a relationship. That now she's convinced I'm only pursuing her because she pulled me out of the plane."

Britney exhaled sharply. "You're just going to have to tell her how you feel. That's all there is to it. You are going to have to risk getting your heart broken."

"I don't know if I can, Brit. The idea that she could—"

"She's in love with you."

"It doesn't matter if I can't convince her that I feel the same way."

Britney flopped back against the chair. "There has to be a way." She took a deep breath. "Did you know Trixie had Harley blacklisted?"

"What? Why?"

"All the vendors will say is that Trixie was the one behind Harley not being able to find a job. That's it."

"She was engaged to Samuel Baldwin."

Britney's eyes widened. "No. That's Sam's Harley? I can't believe I didn't put it together. I mean, yeah, I'm ditzy, but geez, that's even slow for me."

"I didn't know. I knew we were invited, but I never saw the actual invitation. You're the one that told me it was called off. I don't even remember you telling me his fiancée's name."

Britney quickly sat forward. "That slimy rat. What do you wanna bet he's behind it?"

"Why?"

She shrugged. "I don't know, but we can find out and kill two birds with one stone."

"How?"

She leaned a little closer. "We're going to get Sam alone, get him to talk about her, and Harley's going to overhear it."

"How can you possibly make sure she overhears it?"

"Because I'm going to be watching you pull that weasel into the study, and Harley and I are going to stand just outside, listening."

Zach rubbed his knuckles along his jaw. "I don't know. That sounds so out there."

"I know, but I have this feeling her job woes track to Sam."

"This feels wrong."

"How bad do you want Harley?"

"Enough to try anything, no matter how wrong it feels."

Britney winked. "That's exactly right. I like the ring of Harley Wolf. She'll make an excellent sister."

Zach smiled. "I do love her. I don't know what I'm going to do if I can't convince her that I do."

His sister laid her hand on his forearm. "I know you do, Zach. I'll do whatever I can to help."

"Thanks, Britney." He felt broken, and he didn't know why. Harley was still close. It wasn't over, but he felt hopeless. Why did he have to say that to his mom? And why did she have to choose that moment to overhear him? She'd missed the part where he said he loved her. It seemed like everything was working against him. For the first time in his life, he wanted someone, and it felt like he was losing.

CHAPTER 24

"Uh, that dress is a little short, isn't it?" Harley's mom asked as she stared at her.

The day had flown by with all the party prepping. When Britney said she could get a party together in a day, she'd meant it. When you had that kind of money to throw at something, it got done, and fast.

She'd barely even seen Zach most of the day. Between making sure everything was where it was supposed to be and getting ready for the event, her day had been packed.

"I don't know. I like it." Harley tried to sound confident. When she was throwing caution to the wind, she should have considered the draft from the short skirt.

Her mom raised her eyebrows. "If you say so. You're old enough to dress yourself."

"Maybe no one will notice."

Her mom belly laughed. "Honey, that's not possible." She tilted her head and smiled like she knew a secret. "I think you've fallen in love with that young fellow."

"What? No."

"You can't lie to me, Harley. I see the way you are around him."

Harley's shoulders sagged. "He doesn't want a relationship, Mom."

"Are you sure? He seems just as smitten with you as you are him."

"I'm positive. He told me so."

"But you do love him. I'm right about that, aren't I?"

Harley pulled in her bottom lip to keep it from trembling. "I love him with all my heart. He's kind and generous. Loving and sweet. I melt when he smiles at me."

Her mom walked to her and put her arms around her. "I'm sorry, honey."

"It's okay. That's the way it goes, right?"

She leaned back. "Maybe it's not as cut and dry as you think. Maybe he'll surprise you."

Right. Harley wasn't holding her breath. She shook her head to clear it. "It's okay. I mean, I'm going back to Lubbock to start my business. I don't need a relationship right now anyway."

"Sure, honey."

A knock came from the door, and her mom went and opened it.

Zach in a tuxedo. Harley's mouth went dry. Oh boy. He looked like a Greek god. His olive skin stood out against the white of his shirt, and it was tailored to hit every inch of him just right.

"Wow," he said. "You look beautiful, Mrs. Wilson."

"I think we both know who that *wow* was for," she said and winked.

His cheeks turned a bright pink, and he grinned as he cast his gaze to the floor. "Uh."

"I think I'll go find April."

"She's downstairs with Britney, greeting guests."

"Thank you." Her mom cut a glance at her and smiled before walking out the door.

Zach stuffed his hands in the pockets of his slacks. "Harley, you look…words won't do you justice."

She waved him off. "Oh, whatever."

He crossed the room and stopped in front of her. "You look fantastic. The red brings out the gold in your eyes."

"Stop," she said and lowered her gaze.

"You do, and it does." His tone was so firm that she lifted her head and locked eyes with his. She wished he'd stop. The compliments were sweet, but they just made her want him more. He held his arm out to her and smiled. "We have guests to greet."

"You have guests to greet. I'm just the girl who helped plan the party."

"Harley Wilson, you are so much more than that."

She smiled as she hooked her arm in his. "You know, you're very charming."

"I try." He winked.

They walked out of her bedroom to the stairs and descended them. Her heart nearly stopped when Samuel Baldwin and his parents came into view. She'd known they were on the guest list, but she'd hoped with the party being so last minute that they wouldn't be able to come.

Her heart hammered in her chest, and her stomach twisted. She was over him, but seeing him still hurt. His family had treated her so badly, and those feelings of inadequacy surfaced so fast it knocked the wind out of her.

Zach cupped her cheek and made her look at him. "Listen to me. Those people down there are guests in my home. If *any* of them so much as give you an unkind look, I will make them leave. You are with me, and you are worth a hundred times more to me than any of them."

"But they're your friends."

"I pick you over all of them."

Why did he have to say nice things like that? "Zach."

"I mean it." He pressed his lips to her forehead. "You mean more to me than anything."

Because she'd saved his life, not because he loved her. "Sure."

They stopped in the large living room, and Zach smiled at her. "Cocoa Puffs?"

"I thought you might like them. Plus, I wanted to watch these stuffy people eat cereal."

Zach threw his head back and laughed. "Dinner and a show."

"No, *breakfast* for dinner and a show. Add a little *Galaxy Quest*, and we're set."

"Thank you. This is perfect. I hope they aren't all eaten. Maybe I'll sneak down tonight and have a midnight snack."

"I might join you."

"Well, Zach Wolf," Samuel's voice boomed. "I see you made it back alive." He shook Zach's hand and turned his gaze on Harley. "And with a friend. Harley."

"Samuel," Harley said through clenched teeth.

"I see you've attached yourself to another wealthy man." His eyes bored into her.

She furrowed her brows. "What are you talking about?"

"I think you know exactly what I'm talking about."

"Sam, you need stop. Right now."

Sam pulled his gaze from Harley and laughed. "I'm just kidding, Zach. Lighten up."

"Right," Zach said, his lips pinched tight, like that wasn't what he wanted to say at all. He turned to Harley. "I need to talk to Sam. I've got some business to run by him while he's here. I'll be back, okay?"

Harley nodded. "Sure." Her heart sank. It was exactly what she feared. They'd talk, Zach would look at her differently, and she'd leave even more brokenhearted.

Zach and Sam walked toward the hall and disappeared into a room as she stood there watching them go. It made her want to run upstairs, pack, and run away.

"Hey," Britney said and hooked her arm in hers. "Come with me." Zach's sister began pulling her in the same direction Zach and Sam had walked.

"Britney, I don't—"

His sister stopped. "I need you to trust me, okay? Just trust me and listen."

Trust her? With what? They'd been so kind to her that she couldn't say no. Her head bobbed up and down. They walked until they were right outside the room where Zach's and Sam's voices were filtering from. Britney put her fingers to her lips. What on earth was going on?

Harley leaned in and strained to hear what was being said. Zach and Samuel were talking about her. Her face heated, and she pinched her lips. Before she could barge in, Britney grabbed her arm and shook her head, mouthing, "Wait. Just listen."

Fine, she'd listen, and then she'd go in there and set them both straight.

"What business did you need to discuss, Zach?" Sam asked as he stuck his hands in his pockets.

Zach mirrored him. He didn't know how to be sneaky. How was he supposed to get Sam to talk? "I want to know about Harley."

"What about her?"

"Well, we have to watch ourselves, right? Out there, you made it sound like she was a gold digger."

Sam chuckled. "I just wanted to see that look in her eyes."

"Oh, that fire? Yeah. She can be fiery."

"Yeah, in more ways than one."

Zach wanted to deck him, but he kept his temper in check. "Why did you break it off?"

Sam narrowed his eyes and then shrugged. "My father was only going to give me twenty percent of the company. I wanted fifty. I knew they'd never approve of me marrying the likes of her, so I used her to get what I wanted."

It took work for Zach to not grab him around the throat. "Huh. So, you were never interested in her?"

He laughed. "No. I tolerated her, but she wasn't really my type. Can't say I wasn't shocked to see her here and on your arm."

"She saved my life."

"So she was good for both of us, then."

Zach was seething inside. He'd never been a violent guy, but it was taking every ounce of willpower he had not to flatten the guy. "Yeah, I guess so. Did you know she worked for Trixie Tanner?"

"Oh yeah. I got Trix to fire her and then blacklist her. Couldn't have her showing up at parties and ruining them by asking me questions. She whined too much."

"You're a despicable human being," Harley said as she burst into the room. "What kind of man uses someone like that?"

"The kind that sees what he wants and does what it takes to get it," Sam said and smiled.

"You may have billions in your bank account, but you're bankrupt as far as I'm concerned. And to think I valued what your family thought of me. There are pigs in mud with more class than you or your parents."

Britney sauntered in. "I second that opinion."

"I third it," Zach said and held up his phone, showing he'd recorded the conversation. "And I think I'll be giving Trixie a call. I doubt you gave her all the details of your failed relationship. I'm sure once she hears this, she'll be happy to work with Harley again. I'm willing to bet your father would be extremely interested in our conversation. Who knows, maybe our entire circle would like to hear it."

"I should have known. Your family bubbled up from the cesspool, and because you suddenly have more than a couple of nickels to rub together, you think you're on the same level as the rest of us."

Zach shook his head. "Sam, if being on the same level as the rest of you means treating people like you treated Harley, I'll gladly swim around in my cesspool."

"Whatever," he said and walked toward the door, bumping Harley as he went. He glanced over his shoulder at Zach and back to her, his eyes raking her up and down. "He deserves you."

"He's a kind man. A good man. And better than you could ever be."

Britney smiled at Zach and winked. "I'll make sure he can find the front door."

"Thanks," Zach said.

Sam scoffed and walked out of the room with Britney following.

Zach crossed the room and stopped in front of Harley, running his hands down her arms. "Are you okay? I'm so sorry you had to hear me talking like that. It was just an act to get him to admit what he did."

"I know. It's okay. Britney warned me. I had no idea about any of that. I feel so stupid."

"No, don't. Wear it as a badge of honor. You're kind and caring, and you'd never treat anyone like that, so you had no idea someone could be like that." He paused, and then he walked to the door and shut it.

"Harley, we need to talk. I need to tell you how I feel."

CHAPTER 25

*H*arley turned away. "Zach, don't. I appreciate you getting Samuel to admit that, but it doesn't change anything."

"You're right; it doesn't," he said and walked back to her. "It doesn't change how I feel about you at all."

"You don't—"

He put this hand over her mouth. "Stop talking a second."

She nodded, and he dropped his hand.

"I know you overheard me talking to my mom. Telling her I didn't want a relationship."

Why was he doing this? Didn't he know how much it hurt? She didn't need it said again. It was burned into her memory. "Exactly—"

He covered her mouth again. "Do I need to keep my hand over your mouth?"

Harley shook her head, and he removed his hand again.

"I was telling my mom I'd said something stupid."

"What?"

"I'd sealed myself off because I thought it was the only way to keep myself from being hurt, but the only thing it did was make me lonely. I don't want to go back to that. Not now. I love you."

She had to be hearing things. He loved her? "You love me?" The words came out barely above a whisper.

"I love you more than I've ever loved anyone. I love your strength, your intelligence, your humor, your laugh. I love every part of you. Getting stranded with you was the best thing to ever happen to me."

Her heart raced a million miles a minute. He loved her. She'd heard it. Saw his lips move as the words slipped from his mouth. She could feel it too. Her tongue felt glued down, and her knees were shaking.

"Well, aren't you going to say something?" Zach's eyes were searching hers. His lips curved down, and his eyebrows furrowed. "Harley, please say something."

She was elated. All this time, she'd been trying to steel her heart so she could leave him, and now she didn't have to. "I love you too," she finally burst out. "I didn't know how I was going to survive leaving you."

The corners of his mouth quirked up, and the smile went all the way to his eyes. "I don't want you to leave. I want to build a life with you."

Harley threw her arms around his neck. She'd never been happier. Getting left at the altar was only the second-best thing to happen to her. "I can't think of anything I want more."

Zach wrapped his arms around her and nuzzled her neck. "I was hoping you'd say that." He leaned back and cupped her cheek. "I love you."

He touched his lips to hers, and she melted into him. His lips were sweet and soft and warm. Even more so now that she knew he loved her.

Relief coursed through Zach. He'd risked telling Harley he loved her, and he'd been rewarded by hearing the words spoken back to him. She loved him.

She broke the kiss and said, "Would you say it again? I want to hear it again."

"I love you. I'll say it as much as you want me to."

This time she didn't say it with words. She swept her lips across his jaw, nipping at his skin as she did.

When she reached his lips, her mouth hovered a breath away. She softly brushed her lips across his and hovered again. Unlike the last time, he didn't have the ability to withstand the maddening way she kissed him. He cupped the back of her head as he deepened the kiss.

This kiss was so much sweeter, knowing that she loved him and that he'd get to spend his days loving her in return. Zach had no idea how long they held each other and kissed, but it wasn't long enough. It'd never be enough for him.

When she pulled back, her face was flushed, and she smiled. "I haven't kissed you nearly enough, but I think we should probably go back out there."

"I'd rather stay here and kiss you."

"You'd choose me over Cocoa Puffs?" She smiled.

He held her gaze. "I'd choose you over anything, Harley."

EPILOGUE

wo years later...

HARLEY SHIELDED her eyes from the sun as she sat in her poolside lounge with her back against Zach's bare chest. He kissed her neck and circled his arms around her, hugging her close. She still couldn't believe they would soon be celebrating their two-year anniversary as a married couple.

The home they'd picked wasn't too far from his family home. Staying close to grandparents felt like the right move once they'd agreed to move from his downtown penthouse.

"I don't think I've told you how much I love you today," Zach said.

She grinned. He said it all the time, and she loved it. "I don't get tired of hearing it."

"I love you." He kissed her neck again as he rubbed her still-growing belly. "I love you too, little lady." The baby slammed her foot into Zach's hand, and he laughed. "Man, she's feisty like her mom."

"We still haven't picked a name." Her due date was only a month away. "I like Evelyn."

"Or Mackenzie."

"Evelyn Wolf. Mackenzie Wolf."

"We could call her Kenna."

She twisted in the seat. "I love that. Mackenzie and call her Kenna. Where did you come up with that?"

"I don't know. I was looking for names that mean fire. That popped up. I just liked it and thought I'd toss it out there."

"Fire, huh?"

"You're full of fire and strength, and she's going to be just like you."

Harley smiled. "And you. Sweet and kind and loving."

He brushed the back of his hand along her cheek. "The best of both of us, and hopefully only the first."

She kissed him. "I love you."

"I love you too."

Who knew two years ago her life would change so

radically. A crashed plane, a deserted island, and a billionaire did just that, and she couldn't have been happier being stranded with Zach Wolf. Her life was a dream come true.

Leave A Review

∾

Join Bree's List

∾

The Cowboy's Fake Marriage
A Clean Fake Relationship Romance Book One

SNEAK PEEK! THE COWBOY'S FAKE
MARRIAGE CHAPTER 1

In the middle of nowhere, Texas, Grace Maddox was as lost as she'd ever been. Her GPS had sent her who knows where, and now, she was cruising through winding hills on a stretch of road that never seemed to end. And while it was beautiful, lost was lost.

At least she was driving her fiancé's old sixties Mustang, which was fun. She could still remember the first time Bret let her drive it. They'd gone far outside Houston so he could teach her how to drive a stick shift. It was awful. She nearly gave up, but Bret pushed her to keep trying.

Bret would have loved being lost in a place with willow trees and grass so lush it looked fake. Add to it the picture-perfect powder-blue sky, and it was like being in a different world. That was Texas, though. You could go from a packed city to desert-dry to what looked like something out of a rainforest without ever leaving the state.

Only, she didn't have the luxury of being lost or slowing down. Her boss, Yolanda, would kill her if she missed this appointment. Not only did it mean good things for Westhall Interior Designs, it meant Grace might finally get the promotion she'd been working for since she was hired six years ago.

All the late nights, coffee runs, and lack of social life had led to these clients: a rich couple with a house in need of a complete interior makeover. They'd specifically asked for Grace after seeing one of her homes featured at the Abilene Design Show. Granted, that was before she lost Bret, but it was still her design that caught their attention.

What would Bret think? Would he be proud of her? She had to think he would. He was always great about cheering her on. She graduated from college with a business degree, but her passion had been design. Instead of encouraging her to get the corporate job, he'd told her to go for her dream. If it weren't for him, she would've never even had the guts to try.

Rubbing her thumb across her engagement ring,

tears pricked her eyes as she thought about him. It had been eight months, and moving on was proving nearly impossible. To the point that she'd been unable to take her ring off yet. How could she move on when she couldn't get over loving him? It's not like he'd left willingly. He'd been taken from her, and she felt hollow.

By now, she would've been married. They would still be in the honeymoon phase.

She swallowed hard and shook her head. There was no point dwelling on it. How many times had she been told to be thankful for the time she had? That didn't make losing him any easier, but she'd finally pulled out of her funk a few months ago. At only thirty-one, she was determined to live her life. It's what Bret would have wanted anyway.

She pulled the ring off and stuck it in her pocket. This time, she'd do it. She'd take it off and keep it off.

Without warning, a rattling noise came from the engine, and white smoke poured from the hood, yanking her from her thoughts.

"Oh, great."

As she pulled to the side of the road, the car shuddered to a stop and died. She opened the door, got out, and walked to the front of the car. The smoke was even thicker now that she was stopped.

Grace raked her hand through her shoulder-length

hair and twisted around. There were no signs of life anywhere. Would roadside assistance even be able to find her, especially since she didn't know where she was?

She walked to the open car door and leaned across the seat to grab her phone. As she straightened, she sighed. "No bars?" What was she going to do now? With another exasperated sigh, she sat down hard in the driver's seat and leaned her head against the headrest.

"If anyone is listening, I could really use a break."

The blue blur of a pickup whizzed past her. She didn't know how fast they were going, but it had to be more than the 65 mph speed limit she'd been driving.

A moment later, the blue pickup returned, facing her head-on as it stopped a few feet away. An average-height man wearing jeans and a denim button-up got out and approached her. If she were to guess age, based on his tanned, weathered face, she'd put him in his fifties.

"Uh, you need some help?" he asked.

"Um." What did she say? Yeah? This was a great place to run into the wrong person and wind up on a missing persons list. Although, he didn't look like a homicidal maniac. Then again, how would she know?

He smiled. "I swear you're safe with me." Holding up both hands, he chuckled. "See, no weapons."

"You could just be saying that."

He shook his head and put his hands on his hips. "I'm Quincy Bellamy, and I'm guessing you're lost."

Grace chewed her thumb. Indecision gripped her. What should she do? Did she have a choice?

She stood and put the car door between them as she stuffed her phone in the pocket of her navy slacks. "I'm Grace Maddox, and I don't think smoke is supposed to be pouring out of the engine."

His smile was warm as he closed the distance between them. He stopped at the front of the car and took a deep breath. "It's a shot in the dark, but by the smell, I'd say your radiator's busted. If you want, I can give you a ride into town, and you can see about getting your car towed."

This man was the first human she'd seen in hours. What if she turned him down? Or better yet, what were the chances of someone else stopping?

She fanned herself with her hand as sweat began to form along her brow. With as hot as it was, if this man didn't kill her, the heat would. "Okay. Thank you."

"Sure." He nodded his head toward the truck. "Get in."

Grace grabbed her purse and locked the car door before walking to the old seventies pickup. It might not be pretty, but it was running, which was more than she could say for Bret's—her Mustang. She pulled on the door handle, and it didn't budge.

"Oh yeah. I'm sorry. That door is persnickety." Quincy jumped into the pickup and reached across the bench seat to push the door open for her.

Well, if Quincy was a killer, at least she knew she could get out. "Thanks," she said as she got in and shut the door. "I appreciate you giving me a ride."

"No problem." He chuckled. "So, you're lost, huh?"

Grace nodded. "Yeah, I've never been more lost. I know I put the address in my GPS correctly. I don't know what happened."

"Willow Valley isn't what you'd call mapped."

"What? Willow Valley?" That wasn't what she'd put into her GPS. How could she have gotten so turned around? She'd even downloaded the app's newest version before she left home.

Quincy glanced at her. "That's where you are."

"How far is Abilene?"

"You're at least three hours from Abilene."

Her eyes widened. "Three hours?" And a broken-down car. How was she going to make her appointment now? Yolanda was going to kill her, raise her from the dead, and kill her again. And promotion? Forget it. It seemed like the last eight months had been one continual shoe drop after another.

"I take it that's not what you wanted to hear."

Grace shook her head and sighed. "No. I wish I knew what happened."

He shrugged. "I guess someone thought you needed a detour."

She snorted. "I wish they'd asked."

"Would you have said yes?"

"No."

Quincy chuckled. "Then that's why they didn't ask."

"Funny." She rolled her eyes.

"So, where you from?"

"Houston."

"Big city. I stayed there a year one week."

Grace wrinkled her nose. "What?"

"Longest week of my life. I swear those highways and roads were so twisted around that it was like driving on concrete spaghetti."

"Okay, I'll give you that. It's busy, bustling, and crazy, but I love it." Warmth filled her as she smiled, thinking of Bret. The smile faded, and she looked out the window. "Loved it."

Quincy cleared his throat. "Were you going to Abilene to find a new place or…"

She looked at him. "No. I'm an interior designer. I'm supposed to be meeting a client first thing tomorrow to show them what I have planned for their home."

"Uh, well, you may have to postpone that. We don't have a car rental place. We *do* have an excellent mechanic, but it takes a while to get parts sometimes since we're so far out of the way."

Great. She looked down at her phone. Still no bars. "Is there better cell reception in town?"

"Sure, it's better, if by better you mean only slightly better than what you've got now." Quincy brightened.

Grace nodded. Of course. That's how everything in her life was working lately. Her gaze blurred as she turned her attention to the rolling hills zipping by, and the companionable silence lengthened.

"Well, we're here," Quincy said.

She jerked her attention forward, looking out the windshield. How long had it taken to get here? No longer lost in thought, she was wide awake and trying to take in everything as they slowly drove through what she'd call Main Street, USA. It was a cute little town. If it were a cartoon, it would remind her of Radiator Springs. "It's…quaint."

"Is that code for old and small?" He pulled the truck into the parking lot of a gas station and parked. A sign that read *Q. B. Fix-it* was painted on the front of the brick building in black-and-white letters.

She laughed. "Maybe."

He lifted an eyebrow and grinned. "All right, I'll give you that. It's old and small, but the people here are worth gold. Everyone knows everyone, and there's something to be said about a community of people who've got your back."

Grace nodded. "That does sound nice." And it did. Her community consisted of her two sisters, her mom, and her grandfather telling her it was time to move on *all* the time, when they actually took time to talk to her.

As he opened the door, he paused. "By the way, that mechanic I told you about?"

"Yeah?"

"That'd be me." He smiled.

Her mouth dropped open. "Why didn't you check the car when you stopped?"

"It's only ten in the morning and already hot enough to fry eggs on the pavement. I might be small-town, but I'm not stupid."

Grace could give him that. It was hot thirty minutes ago and only seemed to be getting hotter.

She took another look out the window before opening the door and getting out. "How long do you think it'll take to get my car running?"

"I have no idea until I'm sure what's wrong, but you'll be here for at least overnight."

Oh man, this was not what she planned at all. Her shoulders sagged. Yolanda was going to be furious. And she didn't have enough reception to call her and warn her or the clients.

"Is there a place I can stay?" she asked. Maybe they'd have a signal booster or a landline. Something that would give her a way to the outside world.

The way Quincy grinned, it almost made her nervous. "About ten miles from here, there's a bed and breakfast. My nephew, Jackson, runs the place. Let me give him a call, and he can give you a lift while I get your car towed to the shop."

Now she wished she'd been paying attention when they arrived in town. "There aren't any hotels?"

"There's one, but I wouldn't stay there."

The way he scrunched his face made Grace wonder just how bad the hotel could be.

"Okay. I guess I don't have much of a choice." She paused. "Is there any way I could get my suitcase out of my car?"

"I'll bring it by later this afternoon. I'm having dinner with Jackson tonight anyway."

"I appreciate that."

He waved her off like it was no big deal. "Go find yourself something to drink in the store. My treat. It shouldn't take Jackson long to get here."

SNEAK PEEK! THE COWBOY'S FAKE MARRIAGE CHAPTER 2

Sweat dripped down Jackson Bellamy's face as he tugged off his Stetson and rubbed his arm across his forehead. His white tank was soaked. He'd abandoned the checkered button-up hours ago. Normally, he kept it on to protect his shoulders and arms from the sun, but it was too stinkin' hot in the midday sun.

It might be freezing in other parts of the county, but Willow Valley, Texas, was an oven. It was only May, which meant the coming summer was going to be boiling-water hot because of the humidity.

He paused and let his gaze roam over the land that lay before him. It was all his now. When his uncle, Quincy, had passed on claiming the place, the ownership had fallen to him. At first, he'd let the place sit.

One, because there was an age clause, and two, he'd been married.

When he'd brought his wife to the farm, she looked at him like he'd grown two heads. She was a city girl, and city girls had no business in the middle of nowhere with not a manicurist in sight. He could be a cowboy all he wanted, as long as that meant staying in Houston.

For a while, he'd given up on the idea of fixing up the place, but when his marriage had fallen apart a year ago, he returned to Willow Valley to piece himself back together as the divorce finalized. So far, he felt like one of those five-thousand-piece puzzles where half of it was all sky, and he was struggling to find what blue piece went where.

Since then, he'd spent hours working on the house, getting it livable again. So much needed to be done on the place, however, that he'd barely made a dent. His plan for this day had been to figure out what indoor paint to buy for the parlor, but the broken fence couldn't wait any longer. The horses needed better grazing.

When he'd checked on it before, he hadn't noticed the posts were rotten. If he'd known they were bad, he wouldn't have let the horses loose in that pasture. It was the same thing he'd told Don Vickers when the man barged in and raised a ruckus about the animals grazing on his land.

Rolling his shoulders, he tried to loosen the muscles aching from the morning spent digging holes. As he picked up the shovel again, his phone rang. He swiped his arm across his forehead again and answered it. "Hello."

"Hey, buddy," Uncle Quincy said. "You're breathing a little hard, aren't you?"

Jackson dropped his hat back onto his head. "I'm working a little hard."

His uncle laughed. "You're only thirty-one. What's a young man like yourself doing out of breath?"

"Fixing the fence on the second pasture. The horses got out, and Vickers raised cane."

"Oh yeah, if there is such a thing as reincarnation, he's coming back as a mule."

Jackson threw his head back and laughed. It was funny but true. "All right, what did you call for?"

"Got a favor to ask of you."

It was Quincy, so he didn't have the heart to turn him down flat. The man had raised him from the time he was six. "What's that?"

"I got someone who needs a place to stay for the night. Their car broke down just outside of town."

Jackson lifted an eyebrow. "Does this someone happen to be a woman?"

"Now, don't you go giving me any lip. This nice lady needs help. Her Mustang broke down, and I need to fix it."

"Oh really?" Jackson had lost track of the number of times his uncle had set him up with some so-called helpless lady.

"I'm telling the truth. Smoke was billowing from the engine. I'm pretty sure it's the radiator, but until I get under the hood, I won't know for sure."

Right. What had his uncle promised this woman? With the last one, he'd promised a new engine if she'd pretend she needed lodging. "Uh-huh."

"Jackson Bartholomew Bellamy, I'm telling you her car broke down. Now get yourself here and get this poor woman. It's almost lunchtime, and she's going to be hungry. I've got a few sandwiches, but I don't think someone like her will be interested in convenience-store limp-lettuce ham and cheese."

He'd used all three names? Boy, he was desperate this time. "All right, I'll come get her." Sometimes, he wished he had an ornery streak, but his uncle had done too good of a job raising him. He couldn't bring himself to be anything less than a gentleman.

"You're coming now, right?"

"Yep," he said as got into his pickup. "I'm leaving right now."

"Good. I'm going to get her car. You mind your manners, you hear?"

"Yes, sir."

"Good, I'll talk to you later."

"Later," Jackson said and hung up the phone. He shook his head as he started the truck and put it in gear.

Why couldn't his uncle just let him be? Jackson enjoyed his life. Yeah, it was a little lonely, but not so lonely that he needed to be set up by his uncle. Besides, it wasn't that long ago that he was married. Hannah was the love of his life, or so he thought. He'd given every piece of himself to her, and she'd run off and left him shattered. Never would he have thought he'd be in his early thirties and divorced.

It's not that he necessarily *wanted* to be alone, there just wasn't anyone he'd been interested in. Jackson hadn't given up on love; he'd just set his standards higher this time. The next time he got married, he was going to be more careful with who he picked.

A half an hour later, he parked his truck next to his uncle's pickup. Geez, the man tried too hard to be smooth. The tow truck was gone, and Jackson could make out a slender figure in the store. Well, he'd try to let her down easy and hope his uncle hadn't promised too much this time.

He hopped out of the truck and strolled to the door. As the bell above it chimed when he opened it, a woman turned, and wide eyes greeted him. For a second, he was frozen by her beauty, until he remembered it was a setup.

He tipped his hat to her. "I'm Jackson Bellamy."

The woman smiled as she walked toward him. "Hi. I'm Grace Maddox. I'm sorry about this. I never thought to ask your uncle if you had a room available."

He always had plenty of room. The Willow Bend Bed and Breakfast was the star of Central Texas back in the day, but now it was rough inside and out. It was livable, but no one in their right mind would pay top dollar to stay there anymore. Jackson had a lot in common with that house.

"Oh, it's no problem. I've got room." He shook her hand and returned her smile. "So, your car broke down, huh?"

"Yeah, first I get lost, and then my car breaks down." She sighed, and he could have sworn she said, "Of course."

He studied her a moment. Where had his uncle found her? She even sounded sincere, but he'd fallen for that before. The last time was the worst. She'd been a damsel in distress too. Next thing Jackson knew, he was apologizing for his uncle and letting the woman down as easy as he could. Come to find out, Quincy had put his profile up on a farmer's dating website.

Jackson had come unglued when he discovered the truth. After their huge argument, his uncle had promised no more setups, but here he was, being set up yet again. He did have to give it to Quincy. She sure was cute. Her chestnut hair fell to her shoulders in soft waves, little freckles ran across her cheeks and stopped just beyond her hairline over her ears, and she had the cutest button nose of anyone he'd ever seen. It was so perfect that he wondered if it was natural.

"This isn't so bad a place," he said.

"It's bad when you have an appointment to keep and you didn't plan on staying."

He shot her a smile. "Well, how about we get going. I haven't eaten any lunch." He pulled the door open and held it for her. "Have you?"

"Not yet," she said as she passed him.

They walked to Jackson's pickup and got in. He'd left it idling, but the cold air he'd enjoyed on the drive over was lukewarm. "Give the air a second. When we get on the road, it will cool down again."

She nodded and twisted a piece of her hair around her index finger.

He drove about a mile before Grace broke the silence. "You don't look like the owner of a bed and breakfast."

"Oh yeah? What do I look like?" He probably looked a mess after working in the pasture, especially since he didn't grab his button-up and throw it back on.

"Like you should be riding broncos or bulls or roping something."

Jackson let out a chuckle. "Well, I used to, but I gave it up some time ago." He left out the part where his ex-wife was the reason. He'd quit so he could spend more time with Hannah, thinking they could start a family, and he wasn't going to be an absent father—like his dad was.

"Oh, well, it's dangerous, but it's fun to watch." She smiled.

"I agree on both accounts."

She shifted in the seat and crossed her legs. "How long have you lived here?"

He shot her a quick glance. "I was born here."

"How big is the town?"

Jackson snorted. "A little less than five hundred." Which he didn't mind at all. After Hannah, he was hesitant to put himself out there again. He was glad to be back in a place so small because anyone he went to school with was either married, more like a sister, or someone he could never see himself dating.

"Wow. I don't think I could have found a town this size if I'd planned it. What's it like growing up in a place so tiny?"

He shrugged. "I guess it didn't feel so tiny when I little. Where are you from?"

"I was born in Baltimore, but I moved to Houston when I was ten."

"Houston, huh?" He'd lived there a short while with Hannah. He didn't hate the place, but he didn't love it either.

She nodded. "Yeah."

"What brought you this way?" Other than his uncle.

"Uh, I'm an interior designer." She took a deep breath. "Or, well, I should say was. When I call my boss and tell her I've missed the appointment, she'll probably fire me. Which, you know, doesn't make any sense. Like it's my fault my car broke down or that my GPS brought me to the middle of nowhere. Who plans to get lost? And sure, I could have flown to Abilene and then rented a car. But when you've got a '67 Mustang, why wouldn't you want to drive it?" She clamped her lips shut as a blanket of pink covered her cheeks.

Boy, she could talk fast, but he had to admit it was cute. "You get fired up like that a lot?"

"Only when I'm frustrated."

He shot her a smile. "How often are you frustrated?"

Her blush deepened. "Enough that it lands me in hot water sometimes."

"I see."

Grace's knee bounced when silence fell over them and lingered. "Your uncle said the bed and breakfast has been in your family forever."

"It has."

"Would you tell me about it? I love old houses."

He slowed to turn onto the gravel road that led to the place he called home. "Well, you'll see it here in a minute, but it was built in the 1800's. It's been in my family since it was built. Almost a year ago now, I inherited it from my grandfather. He died six years ago, and my uncle held possession of it until I turned thirty. It still needs work, but I plan on making it shine again."

"It sounds great."

Was she serious? "You think so? Most people can't

run away fast enough." And most of those people were of the female persuasion.

The wide smile she gave him made him swallow hard. He had to give it to Quincy. She had a smile that would stop traffic. "I've dreamed of finding an old house and restoring it. There's just something about things built way back when that make them special, ya know?"

"Yeah, I agree."

She twisted in the seat to face him. "Like, they've got these great bones, and all they need is a little love and they'll be as strong as ever. You can't get that nowadays."

Her excitement was contagious, and before he could stop himself, he added, "And the aged wood. You can't fake that kind of thing."

"Oh, I totally agree. I had this one client who bought an old church and was turning it into a residence. He wanted modern everything. I tried my best to get him to reconsider, but, nope, the guy insisted on ripping up the wood floors. I was so mad, but I found a carpenter who took them. He sent me pictures of that wood floor repurposed in a new house. I nearly cried."

As the truck coasted to a stop, he tipped his chin toward the house. "There she is."

Grace steepled her fingers and pressed them to her lips. A small gasp escaped, and she said, "Oh, this is… this is incredible."

A ring on her left finger glinted in the sunlight, and it was like a poke in the eye. Engaged? He hadn't seen a ring when he picked her up. Where had that come from? Jackson was going to give his uncle an earful when he saw him next for trying to set him up with an engaged woman.

Grab your copy of The Cowboy's Fake Marriage to follow Grace and Jackson find their happily-ever-after.

SNEAK PEEK! LOVE AND CHARITY
CHAPTER 2

Maggie Lawrence checked the time on her phone as she stuck her earbuds in. Music always soothed her before a show. In fifteen minutes, some unknown assistant with *The Davis Jones Late Show* would stick their head in the door and tell her it was time to go on.

The green room before the show was the part she loved the best. It gave her a chance to take a deep breath and prepare. She wasn't particularly thrilled with doing the interviews, but she put up with it because being on a live show brought in donations for her Middleman Foundation.

She scooted down in one of six bright red cushy chairs and put her feet up on the coffee table, crossing them at the ankles. At least this time she wasn't sharing space with someone else. Thinking about the last time with that crazy musician made her shiver.

It was weird to think that five years ago she was a housewife slash writer, aching for the opportunity to be on a television show giving an interview. If they knew she was M.G. Law, author of the *Famished* series, the interview would be completely different.

Famished made her a household name, and the quiet anonymity she enjoyed would be wishful thinking if she had done an interview then. It was Mark who had given her the advice to go with a pen name.

Her husband, Mark. The name slammed into her. If she hadn't listened to him, the public would know about the car accident, his death…all of it. She wouldn't be anything other than a widow, and all the questions would come back to that. The thought made it hard to breathe.

The phone in her pocket vibrated, tickling her hip. She pulled it out. Laura, her best friend. What Maggie didn't need right now was a conversation about anything other than her interview and her two-week press junket. She gulped a lungful of air and cleared her throat. "Hey." She hoped her voice didn't betray her.

"Hey, Maggie." Laura sounded cheerful on the other end.

"What's up?" Maggie wound her earbuds up and stuffed them in her wristlet.

"There's been a change of plans while you're in New York."

Great. Not what she wanted to hear. "You know how I feel about change."

"Yeah, but I also know how much you love helping people."

"Fine."

"You were supposed to meet Mrs. Stephens from the Living Hope Foundation, but she had to reschedule."

"And…"

"I received a call from Levi Martin's rep, and he wants to meet you for dinner tonight."

"Oh, really?"

Laura laughed. "He thinks he'll flash a pretty smile and you'll donate to his Geeks for Fibrosis Fan Experience."

Levi Martin had more than a pretty smile. The thirty-eight-year-old actor was gorgeous…dark hair, brown eyes, and modestly built. He usually took roles where he played the loveable goofball. He was in shape, but not so large his head was too small for his body. But lately, he was becoming known more for his wild parties and drinking than the sweet-natured, guy-next-door he used to be.

"Why didn't you just tell him no?"

"I tried, but he wouldn't take no for an answer."

"You sucker." Maggie laughed and looked at her watch again. Five minutes.

"I know it's totally last minute, but Levi is in New York for an audition, and he could fit it in."

"Have you already told him yes?"

Laura paused.

"That would be a *yes*," Maggie said and rolled her eyes.

"Yes."

"All right, when and where?"

"He said he'll have a car waiting for you after your appearance."

"Okay, I'll just tell him no."

"Ruthless."

"Yep." Maggie grinned.

"Um, you know what today is, right?"

"You promised, Laura."

A pregnant pause. "I know, but it's Mark's birthday."

"I know," Maggie whispered and shifted in the chair.

"You need to move on, Mags. It wasn't your fault, and carrying that guilt is making you miserable."

"I'm fine."

"You're completely isolated with no friends at all. I wish I hadn't moved East."

"Greg couldn't turn down that promotion. At least you're in Florida where it's warm."

"Yeah, but I miss you."

"I miss you too."

The door clicked and in popped the show's assistant. She tapped her wrist and smiled enthusiastically.

"Okay, I gotta go. Facetime."

"Promise to call me and tell me everything about Levi."

Maggie paused and reluctantly said, "I promise."

Laura squealed.

If Maggie was honest, the success of her philanthropy started with her friend. Laura first suggested it. It was Laura, the CPA, who volunteered to manage the finances, but it was Maggie who bulldozed through those first few charities and made them change how they operated. She made them take a hard look at how they spent money and whether or not it actually helped people. Maggie became famous and sought after because of her dogged determination to make sure the money her foundation gave away wasn't wasted on exorbitant salaries.

The assistant stopped at the edge of the stage and pointed to the corners of her smiling lips, hinting that it was time to put on a smile and be charming. Maggie closed her eyes, took a deep breath, and pulled herself into the talk-show frame of mind.

Then she heard, "And now, please give a round of applause and welcome for Maggie Lawrence…" Time to be more than just Maggie.

LEVI MARTIN SPLASHED his face with water and studied it in the hotel bathroom mirror. Just a few months ago, he was shooting the series finale of his show and enjoying the idea of a break. In truth, as much as he loved the show, the last three years had been hard.

Amelia's death and then Rachel's affair…both events left him raw and broken. The tension built in his neck and back, and he rolled his head trying to loosen it.

He'd only come to New York for an audition; but somehow, his best friend, Gary, managed to get him actual face time with Maggie Lawrence.

Before he'd gone to her website, he'd pictured an

unattractive, sour-faced woman. He'd been pleasantly surprised by the photo. Unattractive was not a definition he'd apply to her.

Only a couple years younger than he was, the thirty-six-year-old was just his type—beautiful with long chestnut hair, piercing blue eyes, and a heart-shaped face with just the perfect number of freckles across her cheeks and nose. Her picture alone had made his heart race.

Maggie was famous—well, more like infamous—for her charity work. According to her bio, the Middleman Foundation was the result of her own disappointment with charitable donations. Money going to pad wallets instead of helping people.

She might be tough, but Levi was confident he could flash one of his signature smiles and have her ready to write a check. So far, he hadn't met a woman immune to it.

Levi dug his phone out of his jeans pocket, tapped the screen, and lifted it to his ear.

"Speak to me, baby!" Gary joked.

Levi could barely hear him. "Hey, man, how is it?"

"So, so, so awesome. Gecko is on his fifteenth hot dog, and Barker totally barfed."

"No way, man. Barker? Is he out?"

"Yep. Yeager might have a shot this year. Gecko has four hot dogs on him, but he's slowing down."

Levi sighed. "I missed Barker barfing? It's so not fair."

"You had an audition. What was I gonna do in New York? Plus, you're meeting scary charity lady."

"She's not scary. And you could have come with me. It would have been the best-friend thing to do."

"Like I'd miss the Covina Festival? I haven't missed this contest since we moved here. It's, like, a tradition, man."

"Is it really tradition if I'm not there?"

Gary laughed. "Okay, so maybe not as traditional as it should be."

Levi yanked two shirts from his suitcase and let out a sharp breath. "I'm holding up two shirts. Left or right?"

"Eh, left, right, left, right…right."

"Solid blue it is."

"What can I say? I'm good."

Levi slipped the shirt on, buttoned it, and partially tucked it.

"Keep going, man."

"What?"

"All the way in. Remember, Maggie has the ability

to make Geeks bigger and better. You want to impress her."

Levi sighed and finished tucking in his shirt. "Did her CPA tell you what we would need to do?"

"Nah, man. She said Maggie would fill you in. That is if she'll work with you."

"Hey, it's me." Levi quickly glanced at his phone. Thirty minutes.

"By the way, how did the audition go?"

"I love our talks. So ADD."

Gary screamed into the phone. "What?"

"Nothing. I think it went great. I should hear something next month, I think."

"That's good."

Levi remained quiet. Gary didn't need to know that he wasn't excited about the project or the director. "Hey, man, I need to go. See you tomorrow night?"

"Yeah."

Levi heard a click. "Hello?" He looked at the phone. "Nice." More than anything he wished he was with Gary at the Festival, but when an audition for Lou Remick's new film came up, he couldn't pass up the opportunity. Personally, he didn't care for the guy, but his films were always hits. Even his "low budget" films dwarfed most films.

Levi slipped his jacket on and took one last look in the mirror before heading out the door. Being late to meet Maggie Lawrence was the last thing he wanted. If he made a good impression, Geeks for Fibrosis could get the monetary shot in the arm it needed to be huge.

Grab your copy of Love and Charity and follow Levi and Maggie as they work together to fix his charity and fall in love.

OTHER BOOKS BY BREE LIVINGSTON

A Clean Billionaire Romance Series:

Her Pretend Billionaire Boyfriend:
A Clean Billionaire Romance Book One

Her Second Chance Billionaire Sweetheart:
A Clean Billionaire Romance Book Two

Her Broken Billionaire Boss:
A Clean Billionaire Romance Book Three

Her Fake Billionaire Fiancé
A Clean Billionaire Romance Book Four

A Clean Fake Relationship Romance Series:

The Cowboy's Fake Marriage
A Clean Fake Relationship Romance Book One

The Star's Fake Marriage

A Clean Fake Relationship Romance Book Two

A Clean Romance Stand Alone

Love and Charity

Coming in October! Book 3!

The Bodyguards' Fake Marriage

A Clean Fake Relationship Romance Book Three

ABOUT THE AUTHOR

Bree Livingston lives in the West Texas Panhandle with her husband, children, and cats. She'd have a dog, but they took a vote and the cats won. Not in numbers, but attitude. They wouldn't even debate. They just leveled their little beady eyes at her and that was all it took for her to nix getting a dog. Her hobbies include...nothing because she writes all the time.

She loves carbs, but the love ends there. No, that's not true. The love usually winds up on her hips which is why she loves writing romance. The love in the pages of her books are sweet and clean, and they definitely don't add pounds when you step on the scale. Unless of course, you're actually holding a Kindle while you're weighing. Put the Kindle down and try again. Also, the cookie because that could be the problem too. She knows from experience.

Join her mailing list to be the first to find out

publishing news, contests, and more by going to her website at https://breelivingstonwrit.wixsite.com/breelivingston.

facebook.com/BreeLivingstonWrites
twitter.com/BreeLivWrites

Made in the USA
Middletown, DE
05 February 2019